Praise for LAURIE H
"Does *anyone* write troubled tee

This book should be returned to any branch of the
Lancashire County Library on

With her trademark hope, humor, and heart-breaking realism,
Laurie Halse Anderson has given us a roadmap to heal. She is a
treasure" Stephen Chbosky, bestselling author of *THE PERKS
OF BEING A WALLFLOWER*

Praise for PROM
"[Readers] will love Ashley's clear view of high-school
hypocrisies, dating and the fierce bonds of friendship"
BOOKLIST

"This book will delight readers who want their realism
tempered with fun" SCHOOL LIBRARY JOURNAL

"Few adolescent girls will be able to resist Anderson's modern
fairy tale" THE HORN BOOK

Praise for WINTERGIRLS
"Brilliant, intoxicating, full of drama, love and, like the best
books of this kind, hope" Melvin Burgess, OBSERVER

"A fearless, riveting account of a young woman in the grip of a
deadly illness" NEW YORK TIMES

"As difficult as reading this novel can be, it is even more difficult
to put down" PUBLISHERS WEEKLY

"Anderson illuminates a dark but utterly realistic world ... this
is

Lancashire County Library

30118129626176

Praise for TWISTED

"Anderson returns to weightier issues ... and stretches her wings by offering up a male protagonist for the first time"
KIRKUS REVIEWS *Starred Review*

"Tyler truly suffers and the reader suffers with him ... an excellent source of both entertainment and serious conversation" KLIATT *Starred Review*

"Once again, Anderson's taut, confident writing will cause this story to linger long after the book is set down"
SCHOOL LIBRARY JOURNAL

Praise for CATALYST

"Anderson excels in conveying Kate's anxieties ... the universal obstacles she faces and the realistic outcome will likely hold readers' attention" PUBLISHERS WEEKLY

"Intelligently written with multi-dimensional characters that replay in one's mind" KIRKUS REVIEWS

LAURIE HALSE ANDERSON has been published to huge critical acclaim in the United States. Known for tackling tough subjects with humour and sensitivity, her work has earned numerous awards. Two of her books, SPEAK and CHAINS, were National Book Award finalists. CHAINS was also shortlisted for the CILIP Carnegie Medal in the UK. In 2009, Laurie was honoured with the Margaret A. Edwards Award, given by YALSA division of the American Library Association for her "significant and lasting contribution to young adult literature". Mother of four and wife of one, Laurie lives in Northern New York, where she likes to watch the snow fall as she writes.

Visit her at www.madwomanintheforest.com.

Also by Laurie Halse Anderson

Wintergirls
Catalyst
Twisted
Chains
Forge
Speak
Fever 1793

Coming soon
The Impossible Knife of Memory

PROM

LAURIE HALSE ANDERSON

SCHOLASTIC

Scholastic Children's Books
An imprint of Scholastic Ltd
Euston House, 24 Eversholt Street
London, NW1 1DB, UK
Registered office: Westfield Road, Southam, Warwickshire, CV47 0RA
SCHOLASTIC and associated logos are trademarks and/or registered trademarks
of Scholastic Inc.

First published in the US by Viking, a member of Penguin Group (USA) Inc, 2005
This edition published in the UK by Scholastic Ltd, 2014

Copyright © Laurie Halse Anderson, 2005
The right of Laurie Halse Anderson to be identified as the author of this work
has been asserted by her.

ISBN 978 1407 13859 6

A CIP catalogue record for this book is available from the British Library.

All rights reserved.
This book is sold subject to the condition that it shall not, by way of trade or
otherwise, be lent, hired out or otherwise circulated in any form of binding or
cover other than that in which it is published. No part of this publication may be
reproduced, stored in a retrieval system, or transmitted in any form or by any
means (electronic, mechanical, photocopying, recording or otherwise) without the
prior written permission of Scholastic Limited.

Printed and bound by CPI Group (UK) Ltd, Croydon, CRO 4YY
Papers used by Scholastic Children's Books are made from wood grown in
sustainable forests.

1 3 5 7 9 10 8 6 4 2

This is a work of fiction. Names, characters, places, incidents and dialogues are
products of the author's imagination or are used fictitiously. Any resemblance to
actual people, living or dead, events or locales is entirely coincidental.

www.scholastic.co.uk

For Scot,

because every dance is his

Lancashire Library Services	
30118129626176	
PETERS	JF
£7.99	03-Sep-2014
ECO	

1.

Once upon a time there was an eighteen-year-old girl who dragged her butt out of bed and hauled it all the way to school on a sunny day in May.

2.

That was me.

3.

Normal kids (like me) thought high school was cool for the first three days in ninth grade. Then it became a big yawn, the kind of yawn that showed the fillings in your teeth and the white stuff on your tongue you didn't scrape off with your toothbrush.

Sometimes I wondered why I bothered. Normal kids (me

again), we weren't going to college, no matter what anybody said. I could read and write and add and do nails and fix hair and cook a chicken. I could defend myself and knew which streets were cool at night and which neighbourhoods a white girl like me should never, ever wander in.

So why keep showing up for school?

Blame my fifth-grade teacher.

Ms Valencia knew she was teaching a group of normal kids. She knew our parents and our neighbourhood. Couple times a week she'd go off on how we absolutely, positively had to graduate from high school, diploma and all (like the GED didn't count, which was cold), or else we were going straight to hell, with a short detour by Atlantic City to lose all our money in the slot machines. She made an impression, know what I mean?

Every kid who was in that fifth-grade class with me was graduating, except for the three who were in jail, the two who kept having babies, the one who ran away, and the two crack whores.

The rest of us, we were getting by.

I was getting by.

4.

It had been a decent morning, for a Tuesday. No meltdowns at home. The perverts outside the shelter left me alone, and the rottweiler on Seventh was chained up. A bus splashed through the puddle at the corner of Bonventura and Elk, but only my sneakers got soaked. It could have been worse. At least the sun was shining and some of my homework was done.

So I got to admit, I was in a half-decent mood that morning, dragging myself and my butt to school.

I had no clue what was coming.

5.

He was leaning against the telephone pole in front of the building, arms crossed over his chest. His black pants rode dangerous low on his hips. A dark blue hoodie was unzipped to show a faded beater stretched across tight, yummy abs. He had a silver chain around his neck. He needed to shave.

TJ Barnes smiled at me.

"Come here," I said.

6.

Ever kiss someone so hard ... no, not hard, but intense, you know, electric... Ever kiss someone so electric your skin peels off and floats away, and then his skin wraps itself around you to keep you warm and it feels like velvet, and then you look in his eyes and you can see every thought you ever had looking back at you?

TJ did not kiss that good.

But he almost did.

TJ and me met the summer before tenth grade. I was buying a cherry Slurpee at the 7-Eleven. He was bleeding from a broken nose after a fight in the parking lot. I forget what the fight was about. Everybody told me he was trouble, but underneath the trouble he was sweet and fun, and he knew how to make me laugh. Plus, he was hot as hell.

His kiss tasted like cigarettes and toothpaste. I pulled him as close as I could with my clothes on. We hadn't touched each other in, like, four days, and that's a crime when you're eighteen and he's nineteen.

The kiss lasted a long time. When he locked his lips on mine, the whole freaking neighbourhood vanished – *poof!* – in a cloud of bus exhaust. I heated up so fast I dried my sneakers from the inside out.

He was happy to see me, too.

7.

When we stopped kissing, the noise in front of the school started up again: traffic screaming, music ba-booming out of windows, and people giving us shit as they walked by.

"Get a room."

"Get me a piece, TJ!"

I pulled back.

Monica jogged past us, holding on to her earrings so they didn't bounce against her shoulders. "You better hurry, Ash. Bell's gonna ring. Yo, Teej, 'sup?"

TJ nodded once.

"How's it going?" I asked.

"Down to one forty-two this morning." Monica smiled. "Seven more pounds, eleven days. I'ma make it, you watch." She ran for the door.

TJ kissed my neck. "I missed you."

"Missed you, too. Where were you all weekend?"

"Jersey. Helpin' my cousin side a house."

"You know how to side houses?"

"Now I do." His tongue flicked my earlobe. "You tell your parents?"

"Not yet. I worked a double shift Saturday. Sunday I had to babysit. Yesterday was crazy."

"When you gonna tell them?"

"Soon. It has to be the right time, you know."

"Um-hmm." He licked my ear like a Labrador retriever. "Let's get outta here."

"I can't. I got health."

"Blow it off."

"I have too many detentions. I gotta be good."

"Tell Jonesie you had cramps. We'll go to Burger King."

5

Hmmm. I was in the mood for hash browns, maybe a sausage biscuit. "You paying?"

He raised my hand up to his lips and tried to kiss it.

I pulled it away. "Oh, no, you don't. You just worked construction for four days. What happened to the money?"

"I used it for the security deposit. Come on, babe. I'm hungry."

I shouldn't have bitched. The deposit was for an apartment. Our apartment. To live in after I graduated, because no way was I staying home with my family. We had big plans, me and TJ. The apartment was just the beginning. We were going to get our own cars. I wanted to travel, too, to L.A. and Cancun, or the Bahamas or Miami, someplace where the sun was always shining and people looked good in their bathing suits. I needed a better job, for sure. I was thinking I could be an executive, even though I'd have to start out answering phones or something. Or maybe a fashion designer. Or one of those people who decide on which shade of lipstick will be popular.

Whatever. We had a lot ahead of us, me and TJ. Least I could do was feed the boy.

I pulled some bills out of my pocket. I was going to peel off a couple ones, but he took the whole wad. Then his phone rang.

He pocketed the cash, flipped open his phone. "Yo."

"Who is it?" I asked.

He held up one finger to shush me. "No, that's not what

6

the dude said," he told the phone. He turned his back to me and whispered something. I followed him. He waved me off with a nasty frown and a shake of his head.

I looked down like I didn't care. My sneakers had brown spots from the puddle. A couple kids walking to the front door laughed. I knew in my brain they weren't laughing at me, but my stomach said that they thought I was one of those girls waiting, waiting, waiting on her man while he did his business.

I was so not in the mood.

I picked up my backpack and walked.

"Ashley!" yelled my boyfriend who thought his phone was more important than me. "Come back!"

8.

I didn't turn around until I was through the metal detectors.

He was gone.

9.

Carceras High used to be worse. It was so bad when I was a freshman, Ma was talking serious parochial school. But then we got this new principal and a new lady superintendent and they changed a bunch of things and we walked in the first day of tenth grade and we were, like, *Whoa, are we in the right place?* I mean, it was still a high school, still built like a prison, but now at lunch we could choose Pizza Hut or Taco Bell because we had our own food court, and they put in more vending machines.

It used to be a lot worse. Kids were stabbed here, a teacher was raped, and the janitors used to smoke pot under the stage in the auditorium. Then all the changes came, including new security guards. They could be rude; they'd pat down the hot girls when they didn't need to, but people stopped bringing knives. The new custodians (*don't* call them janitors) walked around in uniforms with logos of the companies that sold us cleaning supplies. They never got high during school hours and they kept the toilets flushing.

It used to be way worse.

10.

The halls were solid people.

I had to read a book once for English about a girl, and in the first chapter she freaked out walking through the crowded halls at her school, and I said to myself, *Damn, that girl is stupid*, because I liked the halls when they were crowded, all those words and faces and hair, and the way people smelled, and all the freaky clothes, and the groups of friends, and the way people checked each other out, strutting what they had, but at the same time, all of us carrying books and looking for a sharp pencil or bumming a pen, and trying not to get to class early.

It sounded like flipping through cable late at night:

"...and then he got all in my face, and I was like, yo..."

"...we was down on Columbus..."

"...it's due today?"

"...and then he goes..."

"...she wants a limo..."

"...he does it again, I'm outta there..."

"...Persia went to New York to get the dress..."

"...why do I need a tux, that's what I want to know..."

"...*ayi, chinga tu madre*..."

"...told her, 'Baby you know I love you, it's just that...'"

"...paged him like fifty million times..."

"...it's due today?"

The bell rang. I didn't have time for my locker. I jogged past the cafeteria, turned left by the HERPES HURTS! poster, and walked into Homeroom/Advanced Drug Awareness with Ms Jones-Atkinson.

The room was half filled with seniors gossiping about the hook-ups and break-ups of the long weekend. Ms J-A was reading the *Philadelphia Daily News* and drinking coffee. Behind her on the board she had written:

11 days until Prom (tickets still available!)
23 days until the final (yes, it counts)
32 days until graduation (don't give up now!!!!!!!)

I should have taken TJ to Burger King. Who was he talking to on the phone? Was he lying about the Jersey cousin? Was it the same cousin who stole cars? Better not be. I had rules, standards. No felonies. Was TJ trying to get me to dump him? Was he dumping me?

Not even seven-thirty in the morning and I was already flipping. They shouldn't let boyfriends hang out in front of school. Messed you up.

Nat wasn't in class yet, so I grabbed a seat next to our friend Lauren. She was waving her fingers in the air, talking about this slick guy she met at a club downtown, and how his hips moved, and how the money poured out of his Gucci wallet, and what he thought about her sweet self wrapped in a leather skirt.

I grabbed her right hand and pulled it down. Her nails looked awful. She could say all she wanted about Mr Bling, but if she was so nervous she peeled off her polish like that, then she didn't give up anything. Probably lied about her name. For sure she didn't tell him how old she was.

Lauren pushed her purse across the desk without missing a beat and I dug through it until I found the right red (Vixen). I started the repair job. She was telling us about how she was dancing and he was moving and the music got slow and just as she got to the good stuff, the PA system squeaked and buzzed.

Principal Banks cleared his throat over the speaker and said, "Quiet, please."

My best friend, Nat, Natalia Shulmensky, slid into the seat in front of me. She waved at Ms J-A, who rolled her eyes and reached for her attendance book.

"Prom committee meeting," Nat whispered. She wiggled in her seat. Prom was Nat's drug of choice.

"Listen up to the announcements," Ms J-A said.

I focused on Lauren's hand, making long, steady strokes of colour, not too much, not too little.

"Because of the water main break last week, today is an F day," Banks announced. "Blah blah blahly, blahing, blahed. Blah. Really blah."

I touched up Lauren's pinkie and tilted it in the light, looking for ridges in the polish.

Banks kept blahing. "Seniors – your teachers will distribute a sheet with all graduation requirements. It is your responsibility to review said requirements and comply. All library fines must be paid by the end of next week in order to be eligible for senior activities. Don't be the student who misses out on the fun because of a two-dollar fine."

A couple guys in the back of the room swore.

"Prom tickets are still on sale. Thanks to our committee's hard work, this year's prom promises to be the biggest extravaganza ever. When you walk into the ballroom of the Hotel Bristol, you'll be transported to a fantastic world of happy endings and dreams come true. Your ticket entitles you to a three-course buffet dinner, unlimited beverages, cake, prom favours, and, of course, dancing. Let's make this a night to remember."

Nat was grinning so hard she almost fell off her seat. "I wrote that. Me, all by myself."

"Shut up, Nat," I said.

"Shuttin' up, Ash." She threw a pencil at me. "Loser."

I tossed it back. "Moron."

Banks cleared his throat. "Prom regulations will be distributed next week. Again, today is an F day, not G. Ignorance is not an excuse. And remember, the tassel is worth the hassle."

The speaker squealed and died.

Ms Jones-Atkinson passed out the papers. "Read 'em and weep."

Carceras High Graduation Requirements

1. You must have accumulated twenty-six credits in order to graduate. Credit is granted only for passing grades. To graduate, you must have a minimum of:

   Four (4) English credits
   Four (4) Math credits
   Four (4) Social Studies credits
   Four (4) Physical Education credits
   Three (3) Science credits
   Three (3) Elective credits
   Two (2) World Language credits
   Two (2) Health credits

2. All library fines must be paid in order to participate in Senior Activities.*

3. All inappropriate clothing fines must be paid in order to participate in Senior Activities.*

4. All damages to school property must be paid for in order to participate in Senior Activities.*

5. All detentions must be served (on a timely basis) in order to participate in Senior Activities.*

6. Any senior who earns a suspension or other Category Two (2) Disciplinary Action** from this day forward will be banned from all Senior Activities.*

   *Senior Activities include Class Picnic, Carceras Senior Prom, and all graduation-related activities.

   **Please refer to your Carceras High Official Handbook for details of Disciplinary Actions.

   Mr Banks's paper sponsored by
   Piscataway Paper Products

   "Let Piscataway Save the Day!"™

Ms J-A started class.

She taught us that drugs are bad.

I did a great job on Lauren's nails.

After class, Ms J-A called me up to her desk to yell at me about a quiz she said I missed and an essay she said I didn't hand in. Then she handed me the note from the office that said I had library fines.

I hadn't been in the library since I was a freshman. Was it still in the same place?

Nat was waiting for me in the hall. "Okay, this is serious."

"You're pregnant," I said.

"Ha," she said. "I don't know what kind of purse to buy for prom."

"Oh, God." I started walking.

"No, Ash, really." She ran to catch up with me. "The purse makes a statement. Metallic says 'hot and independent.' Beaded says 'romantic and tender.' So who am I? It's not like I have to worry what Jason thinks, but what about the rest of the world?"

Jason was her so-called date. His dad worked with her dad. Jason and Nat didn't like each other, but they looked good together, and apparently, that was all that counted. I was not a prom-type person and did not care at all, not even a little bit.

Nat and I stopped. In front of us was a crowd, a wall of shouting people clogging up the hall.

"What's up?" Nat asked.

"Hang on." I got up on my tiptoes. "Looks like a fight. Well, it's going to be a fight in a minute if security doesn't get here."

"A good fight or a nasty fight?"

Two white guys were circling around each other, staring, swearing, spitting, daring the other one to throw the first punch.

"A good fight," I said.

Here's the way it worked at our school: as long as the people who were fighting were the same colour, it was cool. If it turned into a race thing, you wanted to get the hell out of there. People talked about "diversity" and crap, but the truth was, nobody knew how to get along. Not for real.

"It's just stupid," I said. "Let's go."

We squeezed and shoved our way along the edge of the crowd. Even though I was almost six inches taller than Nat, I followed her. Nat always knew where she was going.

When the fight was behind us, she repeated her question. "Metallic or beaded? Who do I want to be?"

I wanted to tell her that nobody made a purse that said "Natalia Shulmensky". Nobody could make a purse that weird. Nat and me had lived next to each other since second grade, when her family came here from Russia. I made sure she looked decent – at least some eyeliner, zit concealer, and blush – before she went out in public. She kept me from jumping off the roof when my family went crazy. She helped me babysit my brothers. I helped her babysit her grandmother. She liked penguins, chocolate frosting from a can, sappy poetry, gum, and violin music. I liked TJ. She flirted with dorkdom, but she could be tough, and most people liked her.

Nope, they didn't make purses that could say all that.

Three security guards and Mr Gilroy, the evil vice principal of discipline, galloped down the hall. We pressed ourselves against the lockers so they didn't run us over. Some kids changed direction to follow them, but Nat and me kept walking.

"I think you should get the beaded purse," I said. "You aren't exactly romantic, but you sure as hell are not 'hot and independent', no offence, not the way they mean in those magazines. They mean hot like, 'I'm too good for you, I got my own money, don't be frontin' me.' You're

16

more like, 'Be my boyfriend, I'll make you cookies, come meet my dad,' know what I mean?"

Nat nodded. "Yeah, but Target is having a sixty per cent off sale on their metallics. I'll ask Miss Crane at our meeting today."

"Maybe she'll have a purse you can borrow," I said as a joke.

She nodded, eyes serious. "That would so cool. Good idea, Ash."

We pushed our way up the stairs to the English wing.

"I heard you and TJ had a fight this morning," she said. "I heard you caught him making out with some little slut."

"That slut he was making out with was me, and no, we didn't fight. It was nothing."

"You should dump him."

"You should buy the beaded purse."

"Shut up."

"Shuttin' up. See ya later."

16.

Second period, English 12: American Literary Connections, Basic, was a waste. Mr Fugal yelled at us for not reading this poem by Langston Hughes. It was about a bird.

I liked Fugal at the beginning of the year, but he lost

17

me when he made us read *The Old Man and the Sea*. Birds! Fish! Why couldn't we read about people?

Since nobody knew the stupid bird poem, Fugal told us to take out our persuasive essay outlines. Persuasive essay? Not even the kids who paid attention had a clue what he was talking about. Fugal exploded.

Then the first miracle happened.

A fire drill.

17.

Fire drill rule #1 – find your friends.

Mine were stretched out in the middle of the soccer field. Nat, Jessica, and the other white girls had stripped down to work on their tans. Some of the biracial girls, like Monica, had, too. Lauren liked her colour, dark coffee, and couldn't be bothered to change it.

I put on Nat's sweatshirt and Monica gave me her jacket to cover my legs. My skin did not tan. My skin burned, peeled, and freckled. God did not intend for Irish kids to play in the sun, according to my mother.

Nat opened up a magazine to an article about feather boas. The air smelled like hot Dumpster, Nat's spearmint gum, and the pot being smoked in the alley across the street. I closed my eyes and listened to the prom gossip bouncing back and forth between all the prom-maniacs.

"…because he is sweet."

"'Sweet' is another word for fat…"

"…then Patrick took that baby slut of his…"

"How many calories do french fries have?"

"My dad said I have to take a white guy or…"

"How many calories do they have without salt?"

"Shaun isn't sweet, he's skinny. Ask him…"

"…eight more pounds till the zipper
will go all the way."

"…definitely need a bra with it…"

"…still can't find shoes."

"…you know she'll get wasted…"

"…can't believe it's so close!"

"Are those sirens coming here?"

I opened my eyes.

Three fire trucks pulled up in front of the building. The fireguys dragged their hoses inside. This was not a drill. This was real. Really real. We might be stuck outside for hours.

I could hear my skin frying. I covered my ankles with

19

open textbooks. "I'm gonna get burned if they don't let us in."

"You'd get burned worse in there," Lauren pointed out.

"There isn't any smoke," I said. "I bet a teacher pulled the alarm 'cause he was sick of us."

"Maybe it was that coach," Monica said.

"What coach?" asked Lauren.

Monica said her cousin Lily was in the nurse's office with a bad stomach, and she heard the nurse talking to a secretary about a lot of money being missing from some account. Vendors were calling the school, and the cops were investigating.

I pulled up the hood on the sweatshirt even though it was eighty degrees. My friends argued about which coach was the kind of jackass who would rip off the school like that. I thought about snow.

Eventually, the fireguys came out of the building, rolled up their hoses and drove away. When we went back inside, the Consumer Ed teacher made my girls cover everything back up. They were very anti-sex at Carceras.

18.

Spanish was boring except for the note that got passed around. It said the kid who started the fire was caught on a security camera. He didn't want to take an algebra test,

20

so he lit a roll of toilet paper. Then he felt bad and pulled the alarm.

The security cameras on the second floor actually worked. That's the kind of thing you needed to know to get by.

After Spanish, I had Study Hall. I hid under a desk in the back row and used Lauren's cell phone to call TJ. He never picked up.

I was over being mad at him. I was nervous.

To be honest, I was hungry, too. TJ was right. Breakfast at Burger King had been a good idea. Ma was always saying I should eat toast before I left the house. She was big on toast. If I had eaten toast, maybe I wouldn't have been such a bitch, and then TJ and me could have had a nice time at Burger King with hash browns and a sausage biscuit, and he'd answer his phone.

19.

Nat caught up with Lauren and me outside Study. She heard that the kid who started the fire was a Nazi wacko, and he had wired the whole building to explode when the bell rang at the end of the day. But she didn't think it was true, because if it was, the school district would get sued for making us go to class and all.

We dropped Lauren off at Calculus. She was such a

kick-ass student, she was going to Drexel on a full ride for her brains, not sports.

Nat and me kept walking to the end of the hall, to the class for normal students: Applied Mathematics for Life, aka Slacker Math. It was one step up from Retard Math and one step down from State College Math. It was a million miles and five doors down from Calculus.

Miss Crane was our math teacher, a rookie. Back in the fall, she tried to be our friend by telling us everything that sucked about her life. We had to listen about her college loans and how she had to pay her parents back for her car and how her room-mates both moved out (maybe she bored them to death) and on and on. The only thing that shut her up was when a couple of the guys in class got real interested in her apartment, where it was, did it have a sliding glass door, did she sleep with the windows open, did she sleep nude ... you know.

When she stopped trying to "connect with us" and focused on math, I liked her better. Nat fell in love with her the minute she announced she was the new prom advisor, "because prom is such a magical moment". Nat had a thing for magical moments.

Crane was having a crappy day, I could see that right

22

off. Her hair was flat on her head like a "before" shot in an ad for volumizer spray. She wasn't wearing any foundation, and you could see day-old green eyeliner in the crusty corner of her left eye. She forgot to put on lipstick and she was wearing khakis – khakis! – stretched one size too tight over her thighs, along with a faded red polo shirt.

"What's up with her?" I whispered to Dalinda, sitting in front of me.

Dalinda blew a bubble. "Ashanti Williams has her for homeroom and said she was crying in her cell phone first thing. Maybe she got dumped."

People were sleeping, eating chicken nuggets, listening to music, talking, and doing homework (not math). Big Mike Whelan was chewing a toothbrush. Nat was in the back of the room, nose in another prom magazine.

Crane stood up. Her eyes did not look one hundred per cent focused. Maybe she finally snapped under the pressure of teaching us. Or she was buzzed. Nah, not her. She had been cranky ever since we came back from spring break. She must have snapped. I was kinda bummed. As far as teachers went, Crane wasn't the worst.

She picked up a textbook. "All right, people, that's enough!" *Bam!* She slammed the book on her desk. "Get out a sheet of paper and a pencil. We're having a quiz. No, not a quiz. Quizzes are for babies, and you're always telling me how grown-up you are. A test. Forty per cent of your grade, in fact."

The class moaned. Nat whined that this was not fair. She was always wanting things to be fair, although they never were.

Crane screamed louder. "Shut! Up! The next person who speaks will automatically get an F and be sent to Mr Gilroy."

The only sound was paper being ripped out of notebooks.

Our mouths weren't moving, but our eyes were, blinking and flashing like billboards. Some people were saying, "Bitch is wack," and some people were saying, "Forty per cent?" and some people were saying, "She's high." Nat looked at me, and her grey Russian eyes said, "Something's really wrong." I said back to her, kind of desperate, "I need a pencil." She dug one out of her purse and tossed it to me.

A couple guys in the back of the room didn't get the hint and started talking the old-fashioned way again. Crane handed them passes to Gilroy and pointed to the door. After they left, she scribbled some problems on the board.

"You'd better get started," she said.

The problems were hard. Way hard. I wasn't your A+ kind of student, but I swear she never showed us half of what she was testing us on.

And then it happened.

The second miracle. Two of them in one day – the kind of thing that made you wonder if maybe the priests were telling the truth after all.

24

A knock on the door.

Everybody stopped writing, because if we were lucky it was going to be Gilroy wanting to conference with her in the hall about the students she sent to him, and if they were conferencing in the hall you better believe we were going to conference in the classroom, so we all lifted our pencils from our papers and held our breath.

It was Mr Banks, the principal. He stuck his head in the door and asked Miss Crane if she would come out and talk to him.

Even better.

Except that she didn't go. She didn't answer him or look his way. She slumped in her chair with her eyes on the paper in front of her.

We all put our pencils down. Mr Banks stepped into the room.

"I'm sorry to disturb your class," he said. "But I need to see you, Miss Crane. Now."

Alex Mullins was sitting closest to the door. He stretched his neck to see what was in the hall, then spun around to look at us, his eyes bugging out. Something or somebody was out there.

Crane stared at her desk. A tired lock of hair flopped in front of her eyes and she tucked it behind her ear. Her hand was shaking.

Mr Banks walked over and stood next to her. "Amy."

Since he looked all serious and sad and he used her

first name, I was thinking that maybe she had a death in her family, or maybe somebody ran over her dog and called the school, or maybe they just found out she flunked her graduate school class and she couldn't teach anymore and she knew that was coming, which was why she didn't take a shower that morning and why she had been so bitchy the last couple weeks.

"You're making this harder on yourself," Mr Banks whispered.

We were all holding our breath so we could hear him.

"You need to come with me to my office. We have some questions for you."

Crane was a statue.

Mr Banks turned to the open door and nodded to whoever or whatever was out there. A cop and one of our security guards walked in. Both wearing uniforms. Cop packing her piece. A lady cop. In my math class. A cop here to bust a teacher, not a student.

Crane pulled a tissue from the pink box on her desk and wiped the tears that had started rolling down her pale face. Nat's jaw bounced off the top of her desk. She had figured out the end of this movie but was too shocked to clue anybody in.

Big Mike spoke up. "Mr Banks, you arresting her?"

I crossed my fingers and prayed to the math gods. A bad test grade at that point was going to keep me from getting my diploma on time. Summer school for sure.

Before Mr Banks could think up a lie, the lady cop said, "We just want to ask Miss Crane a few questions. Come on, ma'am. Let's do this the easy way." She slid her hand under Miss Crane's arm. Miss Crane stood up. She let the cop walk her out of the room, followed close by the security guard.

Mr Banks paused and told us to stay in the classroom until the bell rang and he would be sending an aide just as soon as he could find one.

He closed the door on his way out.

We waited until they were down the hall, then we exploded in cheers and screams and high fives and dancing in the aisles. Never in the history of high school had there been a better end to a test.

21.

Nat didn't make any noise. She didn't even laugh when Big Mike used his gut and his fat behind to wipe the problems off the board. She just sat there, frozen, like Crane. I couldn't get a word out of her.

The bell rang. I asked Monica to keep an eye on Nat because I had to go to science. My homework was done for a change.

By the time I got to the lunchroom seventh period, Nat was surrounded by a bunch of zombie girls – staring dead ahead and mouths hanging open.

It was the prom committee.

Somebody moved over so I could plant half a butt cheek on a seat. "Nat?" I waved my hand in front of her face. "Yoo-hoo, anybody home?"

Lauren put her arm around Nat. "She's in shock. We all are."

"Is this about Crane?"

A couple girls sniffed. Lauren nodded her head.

"And? What's going on?"

Lauren took a deep breath and let it all out. "Miss Crane stole the prom money."

"Wait," I said. "I thought that was a coach."

"Nope. Crane."

"You're shitting me. She stole it? How much?"

"They're not sure yet. A lot."

It took a minute to sink in – our math teacher stole the prom money. Wow. How low could you get?

"Hang on," I said. "So you have to cancel the prom?"

Junie wailed and buried her head in her arms.

"Way to go, Hannigan," Lauren said.

"I'm sorry," I said. "Really, I mean it. This sucks."

I had been saying prom was stupid for years, and it

still was, but it was different for them. They had been waiting for ever for this. Dichelle, she lived with a foster family who had nothing, but everybody, even the second cousins, had pitched in to buy her a dress and shoes and a sparkly headband that looked like a beauty-pageant crown, only not as tacky. Junie had been dating the same stand-up man, Charles, since freshman year, and they were the cutest couple on the planet, and he was going into the army right after graduation, and we were all sure he was going to ask her to marry him at prom. Aisha had been working for free at a braiding shop so she could get her hair done. Monica, her mom died of cancer last year – hell, if anyone deserved a dance, it was that girl.

Prom was stupid for me, but not for them, and I wasn't such a butthead that I couldn't see the difference. But I didn't know what to say or do.

"Anybody want a Tastykake?" I asked.

They didn't even look at me.

23.

Rumors about Crane jammed up the food court, making it even slower than usual.

"...put her in cuffs..."

            "...bought a condo in Wildwood..."

29

"…gonna sue…"

"…lost it at the track…"

"…I heard she owes the mob…"

"…bet it went up her nose…"

"…not true…"

"…I heard she bought a new car…"

"…*madre de Dios*…"

"…don't eat those beans before gym, man…"

When I finally got to the register, I used all the change in the bottom of my purse to buy four Tastykakes. I made sure one of them was a Butterscotch Krimpet because that was Nat's favourite.

Back at the table, we split up three of the Kakes, except for Monica because of her dress diet. I put the Krimpet in front of Nat. She didn't reach for it.

That was a bad sign.

Banks came over the PA system. Everybody in the lunchroom shut up. I was hoping the entire staff had been arrested on conspiracy charges and they had to close school on account of a lack of teachers.

"Pardon the interruption. Teachers, please excuse any prom committee members from class immediately for a meeting in my office. Thank you."

That was an even badder sign. A worse sign.

The prom committee cried harder. They hugged each other and smeared makeup on their shirts and chewed Tastykakes and cursed, and finally they stood up, all except for Nat, who hadn't even looked at her special Krimpet.

The girls picked up their books and purses and bunched together in a herd. Nat still hadn't moved.

"A little help, please, Ash," Lauren said.

I put my hand on Nat's arm, the way that lady cop had done to Crane, and gently tugged her to her feet. I put her purse over her shoulder and picked up her books. Before I led her away from the table, I snatched the Krimpet for myself.

24.

Halfway through my last class of the day, Amer Gov, all us seniors had to go to the auditorium for an emergency assembly. It was hot there, and as loud and mean as a club where the headliner act is two hours late because the lead singer is passed out in the dressing room. Boys were itching for a fight, girls were hungry for blood.

Principals should put this on their wall: Don't Mess with Prom.

Our class was the last one there, so I had to take a

front-row seat. Big Mike Whelan tapped my shoulder. He asked me for gum and I said I didn't have any, then he told me that Miss Crane had secretly married a South American drug lord and the prom money bought them new silverware for their house in the Bahamas. The guy next to him, Hoang Tran, said that was stupid. Drug lords got their silverware for free.

The curtains finally opened. Most people cheered, some booed. Natalia and the prom committee sat in folding chairs on the stage. They looked like wrinkled paper dolls. Banks stood in front of the microphone, with Gilroy next to him. Two security guards walked out of the wings and stood at the front corners of the stage. They were already sweating.

Banks tapped the mike. "Quiet, people."

The crowd got louder.

"Listening is an opportunity, people."

A Hacky Sack landed on the stage.

Gilroy grabbed the mike. "You have two seconds to settle down or you don't find out what's going on with your prom. Your choice."

The noise died. I turned around. People were leaning forward in their seats, girls who spent a ton of cash on their dresses, guys who scored really good limos or were pissed that a sure-thing date just blew up.

"That's better. Listen up and be respectful." Gilroy handed the mike to Banks.

Banks kept it short. Miss Crane had been charged with misappropriating (aka stealing) most of the money for our prom. She had been having personal problems (that got a laugh) and the stress of the situation got to be too much.

"Are we going to get our money back?" a boy shouted.

"Is the prom cancelled?" demanded a girl.

Questions flew out of every part of the auditorium: why couldn't there be a prom, how could this happen, could the students sue the district, was Crane out on bail, what did she spend it on, did Mr Boyd steal money from the baseball team, was this whole thing a hoax, wasn't it a law we were owed a prom, was Crane coming back to give the final, did the prom committee pocket any cash, why did our school suck so bad?

Nat slid down in her seat a little. She looked like an eighteen-year-old girl strapped in the electric chair, waiting for the warden to throw the switch.

Banks raised his hands and Gilroy walked to the front edge of the stage. (That's when he saw me, I know it.) The questions quieted down.

Banks said the administration and the prom committee were "exploring their options", which was a fancy way of saying we were screwed. He warned us all not to get emotional. Then he cleared his throat and he apologized.

"I am so sorry that this has happened to you. You all deserve better, much better. I am proud of each one of you in this room. You show up for class, you do your homework, you follow most of the rules, most of the time. Your lives are hard, but you keep showing up, doing what's right, working for a better future. The very least we can do is to make sure you have a prom to celebrate. We will do everything we can to make that happen."

Was he lying? I couldn't tell.

Banks and the committee girls disappeared off the back of the stage and Gilroy took over the microphone, armed with his clipboard. He read off the list of people who had detention, including me.

"If your name was on this list, you need to proceed directly from the auditorium to the cafeteria when the bell rings and sign in for detention. And I see you, Ashley Hannigan. No excuses. You are running out of days to make these up."

Busted. That's why front row seats stink.

"I want everyone to remain seated until the bell. Thank you for your time and attention, ladies and gentlemen."

He walked off. The security guards folded their arms over their bellies and dared us to make them reach for their walkie-talkies.

25.

Is there anything stupider than detention?

No, there is not. Thank you.

The first thing I did when I finally got out of detention was to look for Nat's car. It wasn't in the parking lot. It wasn't crumpled up against any telephone poles, either. That was good. I used a pay phone to call her house, but all I got was a busy signal, over and over and over again. I guessed that was good, too. Either Nat was on the phone sobbing to one of her prom comm friends, or her grandmother was making crank calls to the government again. I hoped it was Nat.

I grabbed a nerd coming out of the building, one of those kids who stays after for fun, and asked him what time it was. He told me and I cursed, and he ran away juggling his books and his backpack and his Mace pocket spray.

Shit. I had missed the bus and was going to be late for work. Third time in a week. Very bad. If my life was a movie, I could hitchhike and get a lift from a nice old grandma who would die the next week and leave me a million dollars in her will because I was polite. But really, if they turned my life into a movie, it'd be a horror/sick comedy/depressed teen/gurl-gonebad flick. Besides, nobody picked up hitchhikers in my neighbourhood. So I was going to be late, and I'd have to scrub toilets or pick the diapers out of the ball pit.

Detention always wrecked everything.

And then ... my knight in shining armour honked.

Okay, so TJ wasn't riding a horse, he was driving his buddy's rusted El Camino, the one with a plastic window and the missing third gear.

"Your ma told me you had to go to work—" he started.

He stopped for a sec because I crawled in and kissed him.

"—and you might need a ride."

Silence ... almost silence, with wet kissing sounds.

"Good idea?" he finally asked.

I buckled my seat belt. "Awesome idea. You're the best and I'm sorry I was a bitch this morning. Now, drive or my boss'll kill me."

He floored it and I grabbed the dash. We tore through the light at Bonventura just as it turned red and didn't hit anything. TJ shifted like a NASCAR driver, so smooth you could hardly tell about the third gear. We made it halfway there before we had to stop at a light that was really, really red.

"Here." TJ tossed a brown paper bag in my lap.

I unrolled it. "What's this?"

"I thought you might be hungry. I made you a sandwich."

A peanut butter and grape jelly sandwich with the peanut butter spread all the way to the edges the way I liked, and cut into two triangles. Hiding underneath the sandwich was a small yellow flower, a marigold.

"*Awwww!*"

"Stop, honey, I can't shift with you in my lap." He tried to sound cranky but he wasn't.

I sat back and ate my perfect sandwich and tucked the marigold in my hair. We only had a couple blocks left. I asked if he could pick me up after work, but he couldn't because the car had to be back by eight. That was cool. We'd have our own car soon enough. He promised not to go out and party, because he was beat and needed to sleep.

We wound up making out so long in front of work I was really, really late, but it was totally worth it.

28.

Once upon a time there was a girl who served pizza in a rat costume.

29.

That was me.

You've probably been inside an EZ-CHEEZ-E, but just in case you are one of the lucky ones, let me describe it to you.

Take a warehouse. Cover up the asbestos with duct tape. Throw paint at the walls. Lay cheap linoleum over the concrete floor. Stick a kitchen out by the back door. Build a plastic gym with tubes and bouncy rooms and a ball pit by the front window. (Do not go near the ball pit. I warn you.)

Fill the left side of the room with arcade games, the louder the better. Cram fifty tables and three hundred chairs into the other half. Now shove ten of those tables together and build a platform against the far wall. That's the EZ-CHEEZ-E Showtime Stage, where they force the waitresses wearing animal costumes – Rompin' Ratty (me), Happy Hamster, Buddy Bunny, Mighty Mole, Helpful Hedgehog, and Pretty Possum – to sing and dance. All for minimum wage.

The rat costume sucked. The fur was matted down like the shag carpet around my grandma's toilet. It smelled like old cheese and mothballs on the outside and sweat – other people's sweat – on the inside. I didn't have to wear the paws, but the head was required – a hollowed-out foam block with fake eyes, felt ears, and wire whiskers. When the head was on, I looked out through the nostrils. Being seen on the floor without your head would get you fired.

It was tempting, let me tell you.

And the tail. I hated that tail. Kids see a rat's tail and they just gotta pull it. So the tail was reinforced with a metal plate, which meant my rear was always drooping. TJ never worried about anybody hitting on me while I was dressed as Rompin' Ratty.

A new Merry Mouse costume was on order. I was hoping they'd give it to me. Merry Mouse had a lightweight head that turned from side to side, fur that sponged clean, a short tail, armpit vents, and a quick-release bathroom flap. When I told Ma how psyched I was about all this, she looked at me funny and said I should not go around telling people that I was excited about being a mouse instead of a rat.

31.

"Hannigan! Table eight is hungry!"

The manager was gone before I could look out my nostrils. *"Ocho!"* shouted the cook.

Happy Hamster, aka Junie from school (who got the cutest costume because she fit into a size two) grabbed my pies. "Hold out your arms," she said.

I put my rat arms out straight and she loaded me up with two pepperoni, one cheese, and one sausage for the birthday girl.

"Wait," I said. "Didn't they order two cheese? *Dos con queso?*"

The cook shook his head. "No. One cheese. Four pizza. You tell me."

"Okay, whatever. Somebody point me at the doors."

Happy Hamster twisted my shoulders until I faced the right direction, then gave me a little push. "Watch your tail."

I romped into the dining room. That's what rats did. Rats romped.

32.

It was mad busy for half an hour because a couple of baseball teams and some obnoxious kids from the suburbs came in, but then it slowed down. The birthday party at table eight was a pain in my tail every five minutes. They sent back three of their pizzas, claimed their soda was flat, and whined that their ice cream had freezer burn.

When I gave the bill to the table eight dad, he lost it, screaming at the top of his lungs that I had screwed up their order and he wasn't going to pay for a thing. His face was red and pig-sweaty.

I wanted to ask him why he was too cheap to pay for his daughter's birthday party, but I couldn't do that, not with his kid and all her friends watching. I told him if I comped him the food, it would come out of my paycheck, and besides, they ate every bite so how bad could it have been?

His wife was trying to get my attention, shaking her head "no" just a little, trying to get me to back off. I knew that if I pushed up the sleeves of her sweater, I'd find black-and-blue marks. He was that kind of guy.

The dad started yelling to a family coming in the front door that they should leave while they could, that EZ-CHEEZ-E was a rip-off. I told the dad that maybe we should talk about this someplace else, that his kid was crying. The dad yelled even louder, telling the whole world that I had ruined his daughter's special day.

My manager knocked over two chairs trying to get to us. While he was trying to calm down the dad, somebody pulled my tail. I turned around to see who it was and knocked over a pitcher of root beer, which flooded the table and poured on my sneakers. I turned around the other way to see what happened and knocked what was left of the birthday cake off the table.

I got sent home early.

Junie stole bus fare for me from the tip jar.

33.

It was almost seven o'clock when the bus let me off at the end of my block.

Technically, we lived just over the city line from Philly. This let our parents pretend the schools were better. It was a decent neighbourhood. The houses were small, but most of them were in good shape. They weren't row houses; each family had its own yard. This was a big deal.

On that quiet, normal street, our house stood out.

Ever seen somebody with nice-looking hands, strong hands, except right on top of the biggest knuckle there's a nasty wart like some kind of mutant cauliflower, and it's oozing, and it has a black hair curling out of it? You know how it makes you feel to see something like that?

My house could make you feel like that.

I took a deep breath. At least there weren't any cop cars out front.

But it was still early.

Hundreds of dead toy soldiers were scattered on the steps and the porch, some melted in battle. Easter lights were still tacked up around the front window, another horrible idea my mother stole from some horrible magazine in her doctor's waiting room. A stack of comic books and a crumpled package of Oreos were on the porch swing.

Don't think it was quiet. Noise tied the house together like duct tape around a busted water heater: TV in the living room, hammering in the basement, a radio somewhere, and, over the top of everything, my parents

42

yelling. Not yelling at each other. No, they were just yelling to be heard.

Welcome home.

34.

Once upon a time there was a girl who was switched at birth.

35.

Me? Please?

36.

No such luck.

37.

I unlocked the front door and went in.

It was still spring, so the living room was a shrine to our baseball team, the Philadelphia Phillies. In the fall, Dad made it into a shrine to the Eagles (football). Winter was always a little weird. We'd get Flyers decorations (hockey), 76ers decorations (basketball), and Christmas decorations (baby Jesus, who was a Philly fan from way back).

My brothers were on the couch. First was Shawn, who was twelve and who stayed out of trouble as long as he had enough junk food. Next to Shawn was Billy, four years old and not quite as big as one of Shawn's thighs. At the far end of the couch, curled up with Harry Potter #5, was Steven, ten, who read because he liked it, not because he had to. Mutt, our deaf, three-legged wonder dog, was stretched out across the boys.

Nobody looked at me when I walked in. The fact that the television was blaring so loudly the walls were shaking probably had something to do with that.

I turned down the television set—

"Hey!" Shawn yelled. "I was watching that!"

"What? I'm sorry I can't hear you because the TV was so loud my ears are ringing!"

Billy giggled.

"What are you watching?"

Steven answered without taking his eyes off the page. "Napoleon's march into Moscow. He invaded Russia in 1812."

"You like this?"

"It's awesome," Shawn said. "Their feet froze and their toes fell off and they kept marching."

"Poor strategy," Steven added.

44

"Isn't it bedtime?"

"It's not even eight," Billy said. "We're not babies. Geez, Ashley."

Shawn chuckled and Steven smiled as he turned the page.

The Three Musketeers, that's what we called them. When they weren't trying to kill each other, they stuck together. Part of me wanted to snuggle with them on the couch, lean up against Shawn, let Billy cuddle with me, and put my feet on Steven's lap, which he would let me do if I put on clean socks first. I'd even let Mutt sit with us.

There was a sound from the basement like a bowling ball being dropped on a mirror, then our father's voice screaming, "Goddamnit! This mother—"

Shawn grabbed the remote and turned up the volume. *Oh.*

"What's he doing down there?" I shouted.

"Cleaning up," Shawn said.

"Swearing," Billy said.

"He's working on your new bedroom," Steven explained. "Remember – you're happy about it."

38.

I picked my way across the living room and around the piles of clothes in the dining room. Dad met me at the top of the basement steps, a grocery bag in his arms. His shirt had pit stains, his jeans were torn at the knee, and there was a cobweb in his beard. My father was not a suit-and-tie guy, not by a long shot. He drove a taxicab and helped out buddies with any kind of under-the-table work he could get. But cobwebs in his beard? That was a new fashion low, even for him.

He leaned against the doorframe.

"Hey, honey. Got pizza?"

"Nope. I'm lucky I still have a job."

"Sucked again, huh?" He shifted the grocery bag to his other arm. It made a tinkling, broken noise.

"What's in there?"

"I sort of dropped that old punch bowl that we never used for anything. But don't tell your mother. You know how she gets."

"Where is she?"

"Hanging laundry."

"Why?"

"Dryer's busted again. The washer doesn't sound too good either. I'll deal with that later. I've gotta finish up your room, princess."

For the past month he had been waiting on drywall, waiting on some wiring, looking for a guy he could score insulation off of. "My room" was another one of his fantasy plans, like the pool for the backyard, the family trip out West, and season tickets behind first base.

But now he was ... sweaty. And there was a cobweb in his beard.

He rubbed his forehead on his sleeve. "You're gonna love it, Ash."

Was he really fixing the basement up? I had to see for myself. I kicked off my sneakers. "I spilled root beer on these. I need to wash them."

He took them from me. "I'll take care of it. Don't want you down there till I'm finished. Go help your mother. That laundry is heavy."

I stared at him for a second, but he wasn't going to budge. I turned to go.

"Oh, I almost forgot," he said. "TJ called."

"When?"

"While you were at work. Told me all about his new job."

"My TJ? Job?"

"Yeah. Seemed happy. Said he'd be home by nine if you want to go over."

"TJ said he has a job?"

"What, we got an echo in here? The boy got a job. About time if you ask me. He's flying straighter these days. I like that. There's meat loaf in the fridge. You hungry?"

"Starved."

Her Royal Highness called as I reached for the meat loaf.

"Ashley? Is that you?"

Swear to God that voice could peel paint.

I crossed the kitchen to the back door.

Ma was hanging sheets on the line. From where I was standing, you might believe Mary Alice Hannigan was a regular mother. She was a little shorter than me, five-six, maybe. She wasn't super-biggie size fat, but she wasn't a starving stick woman either. From the back you might think, *The heels are a little high, and the pants are a little tight, but that hair colour is good, almost as red as Ashley's.* You also might think, *It's a shame she ruins it with that dead poodle tease job on the top of her head. A real shame.*

And then Mary Alice would turn around, and you'd have to cover your mouth with your hand so you didn't say something rude.

The first shock? Let's begin with the belly. The eight-months-and-counting pregnant belly. You'd think that after four kids, she'd have figured out what was causing it. But wait, it gets better. What could be more embarrassing than that belly that screams to the world that your parents keep having sex? Get a load of that hickey on the left side of Ma's neck. First time I brought home a hickey, she sent me to confession. But ever since her and Dad renewed their vows on the boardwalk last summer, she said hickeys are "a sign of affection" instead of a stain of sin.

And the clothes. My mother was frozen in the eighties. Think early Madonna with a watermelon under her shirt. She loved stretch pants, polka dots on her shirts, and earrings the size of cinnamon buns. Add to that her "attractive", "sturdy" city bus–driver shoes, and you want to run in the other direction.

You should.

"Ashley!"

If I wasn't switched at birth, I must have pissed off an evil fairy or something.

40.

I opened the back door.

"Why are you home so soon?" Ma asked. "Is everything okay?"

"Yeah, I had a chance to get off early so I took it."

"That's nice. Turn the light on, will you?"

"It'll attract bugs."

"I need to see."

I flicked the light switch on and walked down the steps to help her. I pulled a Pokémon sheet from the basket and reached for the bucket of clothespins.

"Here, let me do that," Ma said.

"I can pin it."

"You don't pin right."

"I do, too."

"You leave marks when you pin."

I wasn't letting go of that sheet. "Dad said I should help you. This is heavy. You know your back hurts."

She stared, hand on her hip.

"All right. You lift, I'll pin."

We hung a few sheets without talking, then she asked me the real reason I came home early. I filled her in on the ups and downs of my shift ... well, I filled her in on the downs of my shift. I exaggerated a little to make it all sound funny instead of lame and finally got her to laugh. I tried to get her to tell me about her day. Ma drove the 32 bus, Northeast Philly, our neighbourhood, and beyond. She lied through her teeth and said her bus worked perfectly, her seat was comfortable, and her riders all treated her like a goddess.

Next door at Nat's, somebody turned up a radio to blare violin and trumpet music. The back door opened, and Nat's loony grandmother, wearing a bathrobe and her flowered bathing cap, gimped down the stairs, sat in a lawn chair, and talked to the garden gnomes next to their roses.

"She wandered over this afternoon," Ma said. "Just walked in the kitchen like she lived with us. I found her eating ravioli out of a can at the table. Sitting in *my* chair. Eating our ravioli."

Nat's father worked two jobs, and her parents got divorced before they left Russia, so Grandma was on her own a lot.

"She didn't hurt anything, did she?" I handed Ma the second basket of clothespins. "She's real good at sewing. You should put her to work, have her fix the boys' jeans. Maybe she could hang the laundry."

"She'd need a ladder," Ma said. "What she really needs is a nursing home. She's gonna get hurt, mark my words—"

There was a crash inside our house. Shawn screamed that Steven was a imbecile. Steven shouted that if Shawn couldn't spell imbecile, he wasn't allowed to call him one.

"Why aren't they playing outside?" I asked.

"They kept bugging me. I sent them in so I could get some peace." She squeezed the water out of one of her maternity bras. "Did I hear your father break something before you came out?"

I pulled out one of her nightshirts. "I didn't hear anything."

"Liar." She pinned the bra, then the shirt.

I bent over the basket. "I don't know why he's bothering."

"What did you say?"

I held up another sheet. "I don't know why he's doing all this work."

51

"Ashley – duh. You're almost out of high school, for Christ's sake. You can't be crowded in the same bedroom as Billy and the baby. You deserve your own room."

"What if I move out?"

She pinned the sheet fast: boom, boom, boom. "You're not moving out. You're too young."

"When you were my age you were married and already had a baby."

"And you're always telling me how I screwed up my life. Your father is going to a lot of trouble to fix up the basement. Hand me that towel. You should be grateful."

I crossed my arms over my chest. "I didn't ask him to do it. You guys just assumed."

"What? You gonna tell me now you have plans? Going to college? Get real, Ash."

"No, it's just that…"

"What?"

"Don't yell at me. I don't know. I haven't decided yet, that's all."

"What's to decide? You're staying with your family. That's what families are for."

"I don't want to stay here for ever."

"Who said for ever? A year? Two years? You can stay as long as you want. This is your home, Ashley."

"But…"

"But what? You have plans I don't know about? What are you going to do, move in with TJ? There's a little baby

52

at that house, too. You move in with him and it's over. You'll get knocked up, he'll have to take a shitty job he hates to pay the bills, and you'll never, ever get out."

Ma stopped to catch her breath. Nat's grandmother shuffled to the fence that divided our yards, raised her fist, and hollered at us.

"What's she saying?" Ma asked.

"I don't know."

"It's okay, Grandma," Ma said loudly. "Go sit down. Talk to your little friends over there."

Grandma made a hand gesture and spit. She shuffled to the back of their house, pulled out a wading pool, and started filling it with the garden hose.

"Turn that light off, will you?" Ma asked. "It's attracting bugs."

There was no point arguing. I walked up the steps and flicked off the light.

Grandma Shulmensky unbuttoned her robe and dropped it on the ground. Underneath she was wearing her red-flowered swimsuit.

"Bath time again," Ma said. "I don't know what it is with that old lady and water. Where's Natalia? Shouldn't she be home by now?"

I couldn't tell her about the prom being cancelled. Prom was one of those subjects that made my normally cranky, pushy, obnoxious mother into a full-blown wackjob. She had been riding my butt since September to get a

53

dress, get shoes, reserve the limo, blah, blah, blah, and I kept telling her no freaking way was I going to spend a fortune on one night of pretend bullshit, until finally the screaming drove my dad around the bend and he made a law saying we couldn't use the p-word anymore.

"She's at Lauren's working on a project," I said.

Nat's grandmother sat in the little pool, backstroking her arms through the air.

"She's a good kid, Natalia." Ma winced as she tried to yank a heavy blue towel from the basket. "She'll go far. "

The towel came out of the basket all at once. Ma teetered and lost her balance.

As she stumbled, I jumped down the steps.

As she fell, I caught her.

I held on tight and staggered backwards a little. She smelled like laundry soap and bleach and her peach body lotion. She pulled me close, dragging me over the top of her belly so her cheek was against my cheek. The baby kicked between us.

She gave me a loud kiss. "Thanks, peanut."

"You okay?"

She got her feet under her and stood straight. "I'm fine."

"You need to sit down, old lady."

She gave me another kiss before she let me go. "You're right."

Ma sat on the second step from the bottom. I hung up

the rest of the towels and set the laundry basket upside down in front of her so she could prop up her feet. It was quieter now. The television had been turned off inside, and the hammering in the basement had stopped. Nat's grandmother rolled onto her stomach and worked on her breast stroke.

"I'm going to shower," I said.

"Good idea. You smell like cheese."

I stepped around her and went up the stairs. "I'm headed over to TJ's after." I opened the screen door. "You coming in?"

She tilted her head back. "Not yet. I want to look at the stars."

I looked up. You couldn't see shit from our yard.

41.

When I got out of the shower, Dad was reading a bedtime story to Billy. They were stretched out on Billy's mattress, Billy holding Binky Rabbit and Dad with his arm around both of them. The light from my desk was shining on the tops of their heads. They had the exact same colour hair, a mix of honey blond with a little copper red in it.

It didn't make me mushy or anything.

I sat on the end of my bed and reached up for my basket of nail polish supplies. I didn't want to go to TJ's

55

with my toenails looking skanky. I soaked a wad of toilet paper with nail polish remover and went to work on my big toe.

"And then what happened?" Billy asked.

Dad peeked at me over the top of the book.

"And then the wicked brothers yelled at Kenny and called him names and made him eat dog food." Dad turned the page.

"Was it gross dog food?"

"Disgusting," Dad said. Billy grinned and wiggled. "After he ate the dog food, he had to clean the wicked brothers' rooms, and polish their motorcycles and get the video games all set up so the brothers could play them as soon as they came home from Bad Guy School."

"But he couldn't play the games, could he?"

Dad's eyes went all buggy. "Are you kidding me? The wicked brothers had, um, cameras, hidden cameras everywhere in the castle. If Kenny even pretended to play video games, they'd throw him in the dungeon for a week!"

Five toenails were polish-free and I couldn't stand it anymore. "What are you reading to him?"

"It's a fairy tale," Billy said. 'Kenny-ella.'"

"Oh, God."

Dad marked his place in the book with his finger and closed it. "What's wrong?"

"'Kenny-ella'? What the hell is that?"

Billy sighed like I was a moron. "Kenny-ella is the

littlest brother, and he has wicked brothers and a stupid sister, and they all pick on Kenny-ella and make him do the worst jobs in the castle, but what they don't know is that Kenny-ella is really a superhero, and the magic taxicab driver gives him a secret ray gun...."

I held up my hands. "I get the picture. The cabbie is a nice touch."

"Hey. We're reading here. Keep your comments to yourself."

"'Kenny-ella' isn't even a real fairy tale. You're warping his mind."

Billy's chin jutted out and he hugged Binky Rabbit tighter. "We're not warping, we're reading."

"Whatever," I said. I tore off another piece of toilet paper and attacked the other foot.

"Thank you," Dad said. "We're reading. Now where were we?" He opened the book and pretended to scan the page. "Here. When the castle was clean and the motorcycles polished, Kenny went to his bedroom...."

"With no stupid sister in it ..." Billy butted in.

"Which he didn't have to share with his stupid sister," Dad agreed.

"Because his sister had her own castle," I said. "With no wicked brothers or motorcycles or crazy parents."

"Did the sister's castle have any video games?" Billy asked.

"Of course. And a maid, and a cook, and a magic closet

57

that filled with new designer fashions every morning when the sun came up."

"Do you mind?" Dad asked.

Billy sat straight up and bounced a little on his mattress. "And the sister's castle was right next to the brothers' castle, and they all got ice cream whenever they wanted, and they all lived happily ever after. I gotta go pee."

A car without a muffler turned the corner, coughed its way down the street, and parked next door.

"Sounds like Nat—" Dad started.

I was gone.

42.

Grandma opened the front door, still in her dripping suit and bathing cap. She said something I didn't understand and waved for me to follow her. She had known me since I was in second grade, but she always acted like I spoke Russian.

The Shulmensky house was the exact same shape and size as ours, but it felt twice as big, even with books and newspapers piled on the floor and covering the furniture. For one thing, it didn't have extra kids or animals laying around. And it was fancy, like a magazine, with pretty curtains that Grandma sewed and pillows and rugs. The

58

Hannigan house smelled like boys and dog and coffee. The Shulmenskys' smelled like furniture polish, boiled meat, and that weird orange tea they were always drinking.

Grandma dragged me up the stairs to Nat's bedroom. She put her finger to her lips. We leaned towards the closed door and listened.

Nothing. Silence, except for the sound of Grandma's suit dripping on the hall carpet. I tried the handle, but the door was locked.

Oh God, she's already dead. She killed herself over the freakin' prom.

Grandma frowned and yelled something Russian. She could have been saying, "Open up, your best friend is here." On the other hand, it could have been, "America is a great country because of canned ravioli."

There was a murmur inside.

Grandma smacked the door once with her hand and waddled back down the stairs.

The lock turned.

I pushed the door open. "Nattie?"

43.

Nat was sitting at her desk with the phone to her ear and her back turned towards me. She hadn't trashed her room. The animé posters were still on the wall, the scrapbooks neatly stacked on their shelf, her bed was made, and the stuffed penguins were lined up on the pillows in order of size.

"Are you okay?" I asked.

She held one finger up in the air. "Yes," she told the phone. "Can you give me her name?" She wrote in a notebook. "And her phone number?" More writing. "Great, that's wonderful. Thank you so much for your help."

She hung up the phone and spun around in her chair. "What's up?"

Her nose was its normal pale self. Her eyes were not puffy. No tears. It didn't look like she had banged her head against a wall or thrown herself on the ground for an all-out temper tantrum. No rope burns on her neck, no razor marks on her wrists. She looked fine, like nothing had happened.

I laid the back of my hand against her forehead. Her temperature was normal. "Are you medicated?"

She laughed. "What are you talking about? What's up?"

I sat on her bed and held a penguin. "I thought you might be a little upset, seeing as how the most important thing in your world was cancelled today. Hello? The prom?"

"It's not really cancelled. Not yet. Mr Banks encouraged us to find another hotel. He was really supportive."

"I'm confused."

She picked up a thick pink notebook with sparkly stars on it. "Mr Banks gave me Miss Crane's notes, all the suppliers, potential vendors, everything. The prom is on and it's going to rock." As she talked, her voice was going higher and higher until it sounded like she just took a hit of helium.

"But you don't have a hotel yet."

"I'm still working on that."

"And what about food, and the decorations, and a DJ?"

"We're having a big meeting after school tomorrow. You should come."

"You guys started planning for this back in October, Natalia, seven months ago. Seven *months*. You think you're going to pull together a different hotel, different everything in a couple days? Get a grip."

She shoved a pencil in the electric pencil sharpener, checked the point, and put it in the pencil holder. "It would be really fun if you helped me. Really."

"Can't. I'm on my way to TJ's."

She took a cigarette out of the pack on the desk and lit it. "Why? Does he need more money?"

"For your information, he worked all weekend. Construction. He's looking at a union job."

"Bull."

"You calling him a liar?"

She tapped the ash into an ashtray. "Let's just say he exaggerates and leave it at that." She held up the pink

61

planning notebook. "It would be so awesome if you helped me. I mean, you don't have to go, but the behind-the-scenes stuff, it could be a blast. Honest. Cross my heart."

I put down the penguin. "It's just a dance, Nat. Let it go."

She gripped the chair. "*Just* a dance?"

I should have left when I found out she wasn't dead. "Well, yeah. I mean, you love it and all, but for kids like me..."

Nat rolled her chair a few inches closer. "Just a *dance?*"

"A stupid dance." I stood up. "I gotta go. TJ's waiting."

Nat rolled in front of the door to block my way. "No, no, really. I want to hear this. Why is it stupid?"

"You don't want to know."

"Yeah, I do. I totally do."

I took a deep breath. "You wear a pretty dress, buy shoes that don't fit, and pretend for one night that you don't go to Carceras, you don't live around here, you pretend that you have money, that you're a movie star or a rap star, or anything except what you really are which is a poor kid from a broke family going nowhere. It's not real. Jesus, Nat, you're going with a guy you don't even like, somebody you barely know, just so you can act like you're in love for a few hours. You'll wake up the next morning and still be the same old person. Why bother?"

She took a hit on the cigarette, sucking so hard I thought it was going to explode into flame. She blew out the smoke and reached for her phone book.

62

"Go play with your boyfriend," she said.

"Whatever," I answered.

44.

TJ, his sister Becca, and Becca's new baby lived with their aunt Lana in a house that should have been condemned years ago. My family was "no-extra-money-for-nothing" poor. TJ's family was "government-cheese-for-dinner" poor.

When I got there, Aunt Lana was at her second job, tending bar at The Haystack. Becca had no clue where TJ was. She handed me her baby because she had been holding it all day long and her arms were ready to fall off. The baby was seven weeks old. It still didn't have a name.

"Max is nice," I said.

"Max is a dweeb." Becca pointed the remote and switched from MTV to MTV2. "My baby is not a dweeb."

"How 'bout Harley?"

"That's a girl's name."

"No, it's not."

"I knew a girl named Harley down in Avalon."

"Oh."

I shifted her kid to my other hip. "You're sure you don't know where TJ is?"

"The baby and me were taking a nap. I heard him come in. He must have left, right? What about Fire?"

"Not."

"Rock?"

"He's a baby, Becca."

"He won't always be a baby. He needs a strong name." She switched back to MTV. "How about Storm?"

"Storm is a girl in *X-Men*. Didn't you see the movie?"

"Damn. Why are all good names girls' names?"

"You should have had a girl."

"Maybe next time."

Max/Harley/Fire/Rock/Storm wailed like his blanket was on fire. We changed his diaper and tried to feed him and rubbed his stomach and rubbed his back, but he wouldn't stop. I wanted to ask Becca about TJ's so-called job, but she was busy. We put him in a new outfit, but he kept crying.

"If TJ calls, tell him I'm going to the park," I finally said.

Becca could barely hear me with the baby screaming in her ear.

"You should call him Noise," I said.

She nodded her head, but she wasn't looking at me; she was patting her baby's back and rocking back and forth and watching ten skinny girls shaking their things in Snoop Dogg's face on the TV. Snoop Dogg looked skizzle-old, if you ask me.

45.

I knew I should go home. It was after nine. I had homework. My highlights needed touching up. My sheets needed changing. I should apologize to Nat. Ma had chores for me. I had homework.

On the other hand, I missed him. And the last place I wanted to go was home.

If TJ was anywhere, he was probably shooting hoops at Pennhope Park. It only took me fifteen minutes on the bus. The lights were on and the courts were all busy. The bleachers were packed with girls watching ball players and guys watching girls watching ball players, and TJ was sure to be in there somewhere.

I pulled the cord.

46.

He wasn't there. Nobody had seen him. Nobody had talked to him.

I borrowed a cell phone and called him twenty times. No answer.

I just hung out, honest. Did not partake of illegal substances, except for some Budweiser. Did not hook up with anybody. Did not shoot baskets. (Was wearing a skirt and my best flip-flops, and was not going to tempt fate.)

I sat on the bleachers with Moira O'Malley and her cousin Brie and some of their friends from St Cecelia's who I didn't really know but had seen around. I said "yo" and they said "yo" and Brie said "what's up" and I said "boys suck" and she said "no shit, you gonna sit with us?" and I sat.

Moira gave me a warm beer. We watched the game.

Brie asked me if it was true that our principal had gambled our prom money away in Vegas. I said no, my math teacher stole it. They looked disappointed.

Some guys from Mother of Hope came over to where we were sitting. They smelled like summer sweat and hair gel. Brie and the other St Cecelia girls went with them to Burger King to get shakes. Moira didn't want to go 'cause she was waiting on a guy who hadn't shown yet. She and me walked over to the playground, sat on the swings, and talked about Father Nunzio, who taught our CCD class in sixth grade. He was the hottest priest in the diocese. His masses were like boy-band concerts, with all the girls crowded up in the front pews having unholy thoughts.

It got late, then later. The guys playing on the court

were older now, guys with hair on their chests and bags under their eyes. They played without talking.

Moira and me swang and drank, though I couldn't keep up with her, didn't even try. She talked until I thought my ears were going to jump off my head and bury themselves in the dirt. I remembered why we stopped being friends when she went to St Cissy. Motormouth Moira O'Malley. She didn't know when to shut up when she was sober. Drunk, she was even worse.

The guys on the court looked like they were playing underwater, pushing hard through the waves. Sweat poured off their heads, down their backs, and stained the waistbands of their shorts. They fell and got back up, and blood ran with the sweat. Every basket made the chain nets jingle. When they dunked, the rim rattled. I couldn't figure out why they kept playing. It looked like work, like they weren't having any fun, like this was the most serious thing that had ever happened to them, like they had to win this game or the world was going to stop spinning.

A black Escalade pulled up to the kerb, and a couple of spectators strolled over to it. Local drug dealer, open for business. My gut tightened up, and I knew it was time to go. I got Moira to her feet and more or less dragged her home. She was hammered. All that talking made the beer kick in harder, extra oxygen or something.

Nobody answered the doorbell at her house and it

made me sad, but I didn't want to cry, not with Moira O'Malley leaning on me, mumbling about Father Nunzio. I laid her on her side in front of the door so she wouldn't drown if she barfed. I made my way back to the boulevard. There wasn't a bus in sight.

It was a long walk home, but it wasn't too hot or too cold or too scary, and I sort of liked it until the blister on the inside of my left big toe popped. I stopped at an all-night deli for Band-Aids. I also bought three cans of ravioli for Grandma Shulmensky.

48.

My house was one hundred per cent dark and one hundred per cent quiet when I got home. That's how late it was.

I tried TJ's cell again before I went to bed.

This time he answered. He was all "I'm so sorry, baby, you know I love you, please forgive me, I had to help this guy, my phone was dead, don't be mad, I'll make it up to you, I made three hundred bucks, I'm doing all this work for us, say something, Ashley, tell me you love me, it won't happen again..."

I said two choice words and hung up.

I was Sleeping Beauty, Sleeping Budweiser Beauty. Nothing could wake me.

Billy jumped up and down on my behind. I slept.

Shawn put underwear on my head. Kept sleeping.

Mutt crawled in next to me. Bad breath, but not bad enough to kick him out.

Steven left me alone. Probably reading.

Ma hollered at me, but I didn't move. Dad told her to let me sleep it off. When she left the room, he whispered that I should eat some crackers, drink a lot of water, and take aspirin. He left the box of crackers by my bed.

I'd like to point out for the record that I got out of bed, took a shower, brushed my teeth, ate a ton of crackers, drank a quart of orange juice, and made it to school in time for math, fifth period.

Just so you don't think I was a total loser.

I cut math to do my star report, because if I showed up in science without it, I'd be dead, d-e-a-d, call-your-momma-and-cancel-your-graduation-party dead.

You couldn't just sit down and do your homework in peace at Carceras. You needed a pass to get into a study hall or the cafeteria if it wasn't your lunch. I had to dodge security and avoid the halls with the working cameras. I snuck up stairwells and down the back hall like some chick from a James Bond movie, all so I could get to the third-floor girls' bathroom without being busted. That's where I wrote up everything I knew about the constellation Andromeda.

Schools should make it easier for kids who want to do their homework.

Didn't fall asleep in science. Head hurt too much.

Wanted to take a nap during lunch but couldn't, because Ms Jones-Atkinson hunted me down, captured me, and dragged me to her room where she pointed a gun at me and forced me to take the make-up quiz.

Okay, I made up that part about the gun. But the rest was true.

In Amer Gov we studied the Bill of Rights. Somebody pointed out that high school students don't get many of them.

By the end of the day my hangover was gone, but I was still feeling like dirt. I ran into Monica by her locker and asked if she knew where Nat was. She said her weight was stuck at 141.5 and she was very depressed and that Nat was kicking prom butt and taking names. Banks gave her permission to take the day off classes to prepare for the emergency prom meeting.

"You're going, right?"

Monica's eyes hypnotized me like she was a cobra and I was a baby rat. I didn't have a chance.

"Sure," I said. "Wouldn't miss it."

Then she said her brother heard that Miss Crane was having an affair with Mr Banks, and that all sports were going to be cancelled next year because they stole all the extracurricular money.

I told her no way would a young teacher like Crane look twice at a greasy toad like Banks, even if he did have money. She could do better than that.

While we were talking, the loudspeaker read out the detention list. Guess whose name was on it.

"Why do you have so many detentions?" Monica asked.

I had a choice: sit in detention watching the aide pick at her cuticles with a paper clip or go to a prom meeting and make my best friend happy. Detention looked better. Nobody would cry or squeal or complain about the price of silk flowers.

But I walked with Monica to the meeting.

54.

There were exactly six people at Nat's "big meeting", including Monica and me. Monica sat with the other girls in the front row. I took a seat in the back.

Nat and I pretended like we weren't looking at each other. Capris were usually a good choice for her, but that day, with painted bobby pins holding her hair out of her face and a pink T-shirt with a monkey on it, she looked as dorky and lost as she did the first day of second grade.

"Okay, let's get started," she said. "I have good news and bad news."

The door opened, and in walked Banks and Gilroy.

"Natalia, ladies," Banks said. "Hope you don't mind."

Nat's face got all splotchy. "Yes, I mean, no, I mean, have a seat. I was going to come to your office after this anyway."

Banks took the chair from behind the teacher's desk and sat in it.

Gilroy saw me and frowned.

Gilroy liked the "good" kids, people like Nat who joined clubs or Lauren who was real smart or anybody who played varsity anything. Normal kids like me, he hated. If a good kid messed up, he was all "I understand, you're under a lot of pressure, try not to let it happen again, give my best to your parents." When a normal kid got in trouble, the attitude was different: "Thought you could get away with it, why are you wasting our time here, they've reserved a space for you at the penitentiary, you make me sick."

Gilroy took a seat by the door. He turned the desk at an angle so he could stare at me.

"We're sorry to interrupt," Banks said. "Go ahead, Natalia."

Nat fiddled with a bobby pin. "Right. Okay. Like I was saying, there is good news and bad news. The good news is that we have a week and a half to pull this off. A lot of people came up to me today and said they really supported our efforts. Prom is important. People care. We can do it."

Yeah, she was looking at me when she said that.

"And the bad news?" asked Gilroy.

"Um, yeah. I called thirty-five hotels, twelve country clubs, three community centres, and a firehouse. I'm still waiting for the VFW post to return my call."

"And?" asked Banks.

Nat picked up a piece of chalk from the blackboard

73

tray. "They're all booked and besides, we can't afford them with the cash we have left. A couple said we could reserve a date for next year, but I explained that wouldn't help our class because we'd all be graduated by then."

"What about the other vendors that Miss Crane dealt with?"

She tossed the chalk from one hand to the other. "The party store guy hung up on me. The rest either cursed me out or told me they are going to sue the school if they don't get paid."

The door opened again. Lauren and two other girls came in.

"Sorry we're late," Lauren said. "We had an NHS meeting."

Gilroy smiled. "No problem, ladies, we're almost done."

Nat frowned. "I was just telling everybody that we have a lot of work to do."

Gilroy interrupted her. "But you don't have a facility."

"Right."

"No suppliers of decorations."

"Right."

"What about the caterers?"

"They won't return my calls."

"The DJ?"

"Nope."

"The videographer?"

"He laughed at me."

74

"And the suppliers for the gift bags?"

She put the chalk back and rubbed the dust off her hands. "They said we should go pound sand."

Gilroy looked at Banks, who sighed and shook his head. "I was afraid it would come to this," Banks said. "We all owe Natalia a debt of gratitude for her dedication and extra effort, but I'm afraid the odds against her, against this prom, were simply stacked too high."

"But I didn't call everybody yet—" Nat started.

Banks and Gilroy stood up. "I'm sorry, girls," said Banks. "We have to face facts." He cleared his throat and straightened his tie. "We must cancel the prom."

A couple girls cursed. Gilroy's eyes went buggy, but Banks glared, signaling Gilroy to keep his muzzle on. *Bad Gilroy. Don't bite the students.*

Nat started shaking in her sandals. The other girls kept swearing and talking louder and louder and louder. Junie burst into tears.

That's when the third miracle happened.

55.

I raised my hand.

"Excuse me," I said.

Banks walked over to Nat, put his arm around her shoulders, and spoke to her quietly.

Gilroy was reaching for the door, trying to get his boss out of there.

I waved my arm in the air, but nobody noticed. The one time in my life when I wanted to participate, and nobody would pay attention.

"Yo, I got a question here," I said.

Well ... I shouted it.

Actually, I screamed it. "YO! I GOT A QUESTION HERE!"

The talking stopped.

"That's better," I said. "Geez, you guys. We're not done yet. Nat, are we done? Is the meeting over?" I shook my head from side to side to give her a clue.

Nat wiped tears away with the back of her hand. "Um, no?"

"Good. I was thinking about a few things."

Nat sniffed. "Um, okay?"

"Do you have a constructive suggestion, Ashley?" Banks asked.

"Yeah, I do. We could use the gym. For the prom, I mean."

"What?"

"No hotel wants us, we don't have much money; why don't we use the gym?"

Monica turned around in her seat to look at me. "If it's in the gym, it's just a dance, not a prom."

"So you're saying that what makes it a prom is if we spend a ton of money, which we don't have? Pardon my ass, but that's stupid."

Everybody thought about that for half a second, then started arguing and agreeing all at the same time.

"It'd be better than nothing."

"I can't get the money back on my dress."

"Ladies..."

"But the gym smells so nasty."

"Eighth graders have dances in the gym."

"Ladies..."

"If we made it look nice..."

"We don't have a choice."

"It will be so embarrassing..."

"Ladies!"

I caught Nat's eye and pointed to Mr Banks. She quieted everybody down by banging her sandal on the desk.

"Thank you. That's better." She slid her sandal back

on. "First of all, we have to ask the principal – Mr Banks, is there any reason why we can't hold the prom in the gym?"

Banks frowned. "I'll have to check with the legal people, liability issues, you know..."

"Security would be a nightmare," Gilroy said. "We'd have to negotiate with the custodial staff, food service..."

My hand shot up again. It had a mind of its own all of a sudden.

"Yes, Ashley?"

"I don't think we should use our cafeteria staff, no offence."

That got a round of applause.

"What do you suggest?" Banks asked.

"We could cook for ourselves, or get our families to help. My mom's macaroni and cheese is famous in our neighbourhood."

"Or we could just have cookies and stuff," said Monica.

"More liability issues," said Gilroy. "Potential food poisoning."

"You saying my mother can't cook?" I asked.

"Wait, wait," Nat said. "The football boosters make food for football games."

"Good point," Banks said.

"A lot of kids won't go," Lauren said. "They won't think it's a real prom if it's at school."

"I see more negatives than positives in this scenario," said Gilroy.

"I think it's a great idea," Banks said. "I think we should try it."

The committee cheered. Gilroy pouted.

"Don't anybody leave, we have to make up to-do lists," Nat said. "Ash, you're going to help, right?"

"Oh, no, no, no, that won't work," Gilroy said. "Ms Hannigan here has way too many detentions to be able to participate in an extracurricular activity like this."

"How many does she have?" Banks asked.

When Gilroy gave him the number, the girls gasped.

"Are you sure?" I asked. "That sounds a little high to me."

"Are you accusing me of something?"

"Let's reconsider," Banks said. "These girls need all the help they can get. Even convicts get time off for good behaviour."

He laughed.

I didn't. Neither did Gilroy.

"What if we cut her number of detentions in half?" Banks suggested. "With the requirement that she help the committee every day."

"That would be great!" Nat chirped.

Gilroy's eyes reminded me of a ferret we used to have. It liked to bite, too. "A noble idea, Mr Banks, but contrary to district policy. The board wants us to enforce a 'no exceptions' discipline. If we let Miss Hannigan off the hook for her infractions, we set a dangerous precedent. I'm sure she understands."

"But, but…" Nat said.

I wanted to pick up Gilroy by his smelly ferret tail and dangle him out the window.

"I see your point," Banks said. "We're sorry, Ashley. You earn detention, you serve detention."

Gilroy opened the door. "That's the way things work in the real world."

We were on the third floor. If I was dangling a ferret out the window and it tried to bite me, I'd drop it.

Nat grabbed Mr Banks's sleeve. "But she can still help, can't she? I mean, as long as she does her detentions, too."

"You said we need all the help we can get," Lauren said.

"I don't see a problem with that," Banks said. "Do you, Mr Gilroy? I think it shows character, to help out friends in need. What do you say, Ashley?"

Everybody turned and stared at me.

Like I had a choice.

57.

My so-called "knight in rusting armour" was not waiting for me after school. Not that I expected him or anything. Jerk.

Nat said she'd drive me to work. We stopped at my house first 'cause I wanted to change. Before I opened the front door, I put my finger in her face.

"Do not, I repeat, do not, say anything about the prom. Don't even say the word 'prom.' Promise me."

Nat rolled her eyes. "Promise."

My brothers and father and dog were in the kitchen. Dad was dressed for a softball game: dirty cleats, tube socks, bright red shorts, and a tank top that showed too much hairy back. He was using tongs to pluck hot dogs out of a giant pot of boiling water. Mutt was spinning in the middle of the floor, his spit flying through the air like Silly String.

So far, so good, you're thinking. All-American dad cooking All-American food. Hungry dog freaking out.

Think again.

Dad waved a steaming hot dog in the air, shouted, "Pop fly!" and threw it across the kitchen. Mutt jumped and missed.

"I got it," Shawn screamed. He reached over Mutt and caught the hot dog in his glove. But the play wasn't over. "First base!" he hollered.

Steven, his nose in a book at the table, flopped open his glove. Shawn tossed the hot dog high, but Steven looked up in time, stretched, and snagged it before it smashed into the window screen. Mutt sprinted towards Steven, hit the brakes too late, and slid into the wall.

"Ouch," Nat said.

"Look out!" shouted Dad. "Runner stealing home!"

Steven put his elbow on his book so he didn't lose his place, picked up the hot dog with his right hand, and threw it back across the kitchen to Dad who caught it and handed it to Billy, standing on a chair next to him.

"We got 'im!" Dad said.

"We got 'im!" Billy squealed.

Mutt shook his head, turned once in a circle, and lay down.

I turned to Nat. "And you wonder why I want to move out?"

Dad reached in the pot. "Give your sister a glove, Shawn. Ash – go long."

"Time out." I teed up my hands. "Where's Ma?"

"At Aunt Linny's," Steven said. "She won't be home for hours."

Billy waved his arms. "She won't be home for hours!" His hot dog snapped in two, and the top piece fell to the floor. Mutt was on it in a flash.

"Time in!" Dad lobbed a dog at me. "Catch!"

Damn thing was hot. I bobbled it twice, then tossed it to Shawn, who flipped it to Steven, who took a bite out of it before he threw it at Billy. Billy caught it in both hands, stuck it in a smushed-up bun, laid down a line of mustard and offered it up to me. "Hungry?"

"What is going on here?" I asked.

"Softball game tonight," Dad said. "Cabbies against the roofers."

Shawn grinned. "Dad's team is gonna get crushed. You coming to watch?"

"Can't," I said. "I have to work until ten."

"Your loss," Dad said. "Hot dog, Nat?"

"I'd love one, Mr Hannigan."

I shook my head. "Eat that at your own risk. It'll take me two seconds to get changed."

58.

My room was over the kitchen, so I could hear them babble. Dad asked Nat if there was any more news about our thieving math teacher, and Nat filled him in. I had just pulled off my shirt when she explained how I was helping with the new prom.

"Shut up!" I grabbed my clothes and ran down the stairs. "Shuttin' up, Nattie, for real!" I skidded into the kitchen pulling on a clean T-shirt. "You swore you wouldn't say that word!"

"Is it true?" Dad asked. "You really going to the prom after all?"

I stepped into one leg of my jeans. "Read these lips: I am not going to the prom."

"She's just helping," Nat explained.

Dad spread relish on a hot dog. "Helping? Like what, serving punch?"

Billy hit Steven's arm. "Punch," he said.

Steven took a bite out of Billy's hot dog. "Bite."

Billy leaned over to bite Steven. Dad grabbed Billy's collar, pulled him off Steven and handed him another hot dog. Mutt sat up and whined and Dad tossed him a bun.

I pulled up my jeans and zipped them. "Nobody drinks punch anymore. I'm just helping with ... what was it you said?"

"Organizational details," Nat said.

"Yeah, that."

"Cool," Dad said. "You gonna need a limo? I know a guy down in Fishtown, he owes me, has classic cars and limos in his fleet. Your ma is going to flip about the dress. God knows that woman can shop. I suppose you'll need shoes, too. The strappy kind you can dance in. Your mother loves those."

"No dress. No shoes. I don't dance." I buckled my belt. "I am just helping. And get this – nobody, and I mean nobody, is going to tell Ma. If she finds out I'm helping with this dance—"

"It's not a *dance*, it's the *prom*," Nat said.

"—with this dance, she'll flip. She'll have such a fit about dresses and flowers and shoes and limos and food and hair and fifty million other stupid things that she will have her baby right here in the kitchen, in front of everybody. Trust me, that is one kind of gross you don't want to see."

"Ew." Shawn put down his hot dog.

"Serious ew," I said. "Think about last year, Dad, when you renewed your vows. It got so bad around here you almost divorced. When it comes to this celebration stuff, she's out of control."

Dad stroked his beard. "You have a point, princess." He jogged towards the living room. "Hang on, I know what to do!"

I took a freshly boiled hot dog out of the pot and stuck it in a clean bun. Mutt licked my ankle and I pushed him away. "You have no idea the bullet we just dodged," I told Nat.

Dad came back holding a thick book. "We'll swear on this. Like a holy oath."

Nat read the title. "You guys swear on *The Lord of the Rings*?"

"I couldn't find the Bible."

Steven stuck a piece of hot dog roll in his book to mark his place. "For some people, *The Lord of the Rings* is holy, too."

The boys gathered around, each one with a hand on the book.

"We swear that we won't say a word," Dad said.

"We swear that we won't say a word," my brothers repeated.

"About the prom to Mary Alice."

"About the prom to Mary Alice."

"No, I mean, to Mom."

"No, I mean, to Mom."

"So help me God and Tug McGraw."

"So help me God and Tug McGraw."

"All right then, men. Let's crush the roofers!"

59.

I had one question rattling around my head the whole time at work.

What was I thinking?

I took orders, delivered them to the kitchen, served flat soda and undercooked pizza, smiled, danced, cleaned tables, mopped floors, and danced some more, a confused rat on cruise control.

What was I thinking!?

No way could I help with the prom. I had a million detentions to serve and was behind in most my classes. I had to go to work and help Ma at home. And I had a social life, sort of, if I was still speaking to TJ and he was still speaking to me.

What the hell was I thinking???

I messed up three orders and spent fifteen minutes switching pizzas from one table to the other. My manager made me mop the floors.

Why did I raise my hand in that meeting? Could I blame my hangover?

Maybe.

Was I just trying to piss off Gilroy?

Probably.

Did this prove that bad things happened when you raised your hand in school?

Absolutely.

60.

When I came home, Mutt was stretched the entire length of the couch, his belly fat with hot dogs and buns. Something was up. The house was too quiet for ten-thirty at night and the dog never got the couch to himself.

"Ma?"

"In the kitchen, Ash," Dad called.

He was on his knees behind the kitchen table, scrubbing the wallpaper in his softball clothes.

"What are you doing?" I asked.

He dipped the scrub brush in a bowl of soapy water. "Cleaning up."

I looked him over for bruises. "Did you get hit on the head?"

He muscled out a red spot on the wall. "After you and

Nat left, we had a little food fight. See that yellow by the window? That's mustard. This is ketchup, obviously."

"What's the green?"

"Relish. But I don't know about the brown stuff."

"Chocolate pudding," I said. "From the craving Ma had at Easter, remember?"

"That's right. I forgot."

I took an orange soda out of the fridge. "How was the game?"

He started on a huge ketchup stain. "We got robbed. The freaking roofers paid off the umpire. What do you expect? I had a couple good hits, though. Sent one out of the park."

"Good for you."

I took a long drink. The only sound in the house was the wet brush on the wall. The wallpaper was coming off and the drywall was dissolving, but the stain was still there.

"TJ called," Dad said.

"I'm not talking to him."

"How come?"

"He stood me up last night."

"Then who were you out with last night?"

"Moira O'Malley. At the park."

"You got drunk at the park without your boyfriend there to protect you?" Dad stopped scrubbing and stared at me. "That was stupid, Ashley Marie. Stupid and dangerous. You coulda got in all kinds of trouble."

88

"Yeah, whatever," I said. "I won't do it again."

"Better not." He picked soggy bits of wallpaper from the brush. "And you should cut TJ some slack."

"I'll think about it. Where is Ma?"

"She's, ah, spending the night at Linny's."

"Why?" I put down the soda. "She's not in labour, is she?"

"No such luck." A piece of wallpaper slid down the wall. "Damn."

"So why is she at Aunt Linny's?"

He tossed the scrub brush in the bowl. Water sloshed over the side and dripped on the floor. Dad pulled out a chair and sat down across from me. "She's a little irritated, with, um ..."

"She's pissed because you guys totally trashed the kitchen."

"You could say that."

"Ma went nuclear."

"Pretty much, yeah. She went to Linny's to cool down. It might take a few days."

I pushed my soda across to him. He chugged it and tossed the can in the trash.

"Sucks to be you."

He got up, opened the utensil drawer, and pulled out all the big spoons. "I'm sorry, princess."

"Why? It's not my kitchen."

He took a spatula out of the drawer and dumped the spoons back in. "Not about this, about your bedroom."

"They trashed my room, too?"

He held up the spatula. The handle was bent. "No, your new room. Downstairs. Fixing this is going to take a while."

"Fixing that spatula?"

"No. The kitchen." He used the spatula to scrape off a piece of wallpaper. "When I'm done stripping this, I'm going to give it a coat of primer and then paint it. Then I'll have to do the rest of the kitchen so it matches, or your mother will have my head on a platter. Your room ain't gonna be done before the baby shows up. That's what I'm sorry for."

"Don't worry about it. I was thinking maybe I could look for an apartment or something."

He snorted. "That's a good one, Ash. You, out on your own." He pulled the trash can closer. "You feel like helping me get this paper off?"

"Not really."

"So that means you'll get your brothers ready for school in the morning."

"You're worse than Ma, you know that?" I put my hand out for the spatula. "Give me that thing."

By the time we were done, the wall looked like it had been through a car wash. Dad said he knew a guy who knew a guy who could get him some primer for cheap. I said whatever, I needed some sleep, and it was after midnight.

I woke up in the middle of an earthquake. No, wait. Not an earthquake. Natalia Shulmensky, flipped-out best friend, was shaking me like the house was on fire.

"You." *Shake.* "Have." *Shake.* "To." *Shake.* "Get." *Shake.* "Up." *Shake.* "Now."

"Go away."

"We." *Shake.* "Have." *Shake.* "To." *Shake.* "Go." She shined a flashlight in my eyes.

"You're crazy. Good night."

"Come." *Shake.* "On." *Shake.* "Ow!"

I smacked her hands and sat up. "What time is it?"

"Time to go."

I uncrossed my eyes and looked at Billy's Spider-Man alarm clock. "It's quarter to five! In the freakin' morning!"

Billy moaned in his sleep.

"Be quiet," Nat hissed. "You'll wake him up."

"I'll wake him up? *I'll* wake him up? Nattie, you know I love you, but I need to kill you right now."

Billy sat up. "Ashley?"

Nat turned off the flashlight and crouched next to my bed.

"Sorry I woke you, Billy-boy." I gave Nat a little kick. "Go back to sleep, honey."

Billy flopped back on his pillow.

Nat handed me a pair of sweatpants from the pile of

almost-dirty clothes on the floor. "I'll explain in the car," she whispered.

I pulled on the sweats. "You're acting like your grandmother, you know."

"What's wrong with that?"

"She's crazy."

"She's not as crazy as you think. Come on."

62.

As soon as I buckled my seat belt, Nat handed me a cup of coffee with a lid and a funky-looking pastry that smelled like a Cinnabon, only it didn't have any icing.

"You're bribing me."

"Yes." She pumped her accelerator and started the car. The engine bucked and coughed loudly and finally turned over.

I took a bite and then I took another bite. Wow. It was amazing; butter, some kind of nuts – walnuts? – sugar, but not too much...

"Like it?" Nat asked.

"'S all right." I sipped my coffee, which she had doctored up exactly the way I liked it. "You're on a roll, aren't you? Breaking and entering, kidnapping, and bribery all before the sun is up."

Nat lit a cigarette, put the car in gear, and pulled away

from the kerb. "Desperate times call for desperate measures." She watched me take a huge bite. "There's more in back if you want."

I turned around. Layers of pastries separated by wax paper were stacked in two cardboard boxes on the backseat. "Where'd those come from?"

"My grandma baked them. Eat up and look in the pink notebook. I wrote out a list for you."

63.

She started me out with an easy job: delivering bribes, I mean the pastry. First stop: the custodians.

They were hanging in their "office", a workshop next to the loading dock. Three guys were playing poker, one was dead asleep on the couch, and the head custodian, an old black guy with a shaved head and thick glasses, was fixing a broken push broom. The radio played Sinatra.

"Yeah?" asked the guy with the biggest pile of chips.

I wanted to drop the pastry box and run. If I did, Nat would wake me up even earlier the next day.

"Yo," I said. "I'm Ashley. I brought breakfast."

They weren't going to argue with that. I handed out the goodies and chatted them up the way my dad did when he wanted to put the squeeze on somebody. One of the guys remembered my family from a Beef 'n' Beer we went to at the VFW with my uncle Danny. Turned out that he and Danny were in the Reserves together. Score another point for Team Hannigan.

The boss guy didn't eat any pastry. The whole time I was yakking, he stood on the other side of the room, wrapping duct tape around the broom handle.

"Hey, little girl," he finally said. "These boys got work to do. What do you want?"

Don't screw this up. "You heard about the prom?"

"They cancelled it," said the boss. "That young math teacher stole all the money."

The guy who was winning the card game cracked up. "math teacher."

"It's not funny," I said.

The boss sliced through the duct tape with silver scissors. "We got nothing to do with the prom."

I swallowed hard. "Yeah, you do. I hope. Let me explain."

64.

By the time I left, we had a deal. They wanted an under-the-table cash bonus and more pastry the night of the prom, but they'd come early and stay late and wouldn't bitch to the administration as long as they didn't have to mop up any beer puke. Couldn't blame them for that.

My second job on my list was scarier. "Chaperones – confirm English teachers."

Ugh.

Why did the chaperones have to be English teachers, you ask? Nat said that English teachers believed in true romance and happy endings, plus none of them coached sports teams.

Okay, that made sense.

But would they listen to me? I had a bad reputation with the English department on account of I hated to read. They were so picky about the reading thing. I don't know why. All the good books get made into movies. They could save themselves a lot of work if they would just show movies in class.

I was pretty sure I wouldn't get a standing ovation when I barged into their office. On the other hand, English teachers liked to eat, just like normal people and custodians.

The English office was basically a big closet without any windows. The walls were totally covered by bulletin boards buried under four inches of tacked-up papers. Eight English teachers sat around the long table that took up most of the room. They were all reading. What a shock.

I cleared my throat, but nobody looked up. They just stared at their books or their newspapers, turned the pages, and stared some more. Was there a special Englishy-password I needed to use? Maybe they didn't speak to students until they were on the clock.

I stood there looking like a total putz until Ms Neary, who gave me a D+ on my *Our Town* poster in ninth grade, put her book down and said, "Is there something wrong, Ashley?"

"Umm, I want to talk to youse about the prom," I said. (Bad start. These were English teachers. I should talk right.) "I mean, I would like to talk with you, all of you, you all, about the prom."

The cute guy teacher who had played basketball at Villanova lowered his newspaper. His hair was still wet from the shower. Made me wish for a second there that I was interested in World Lit or Amer Lit Heroes, because he taught them.

"Prom's back on?" he asked.

"We think so," I said. "But we need your help. Want some pastry? They're killer."

Nat was right. Once the sugar kicked in, the English teachers were nice as could be.

65.

The third item on my list was a meeting with Vice Principal Gilroy to discuss security.

That had to wait. Now that I was a Goody Two-Shoes, I had to go to class.

Our math sub was an oldish guy with grey hair that was too long in the way that let you know his wife dumped him and he was trolling for a girlfriend. He told us he gave up his career as an insurance agent to become a teacher because he wanted to give something back.

Why he thought being a math sub gave anything back to anybody was beyond me.

He asked us what we were studying. Twenty people gave twenty different answers. He offered to calculate how much life insurance we should have. That didn't go down too good. Finally he said if we were quiet, we could do whatever we wanted.

Big Mike raised his hand and asked for a pass so he could go to the nurse. Said he was having ligament problems in his knee. The sub asked how he hurt himself, and Big Mike said it was a football injury. This could have been true, because Big Mike played football in middle school, but I heard he hurt his knee stealing a keg from a frat party. The sub wrote the pass.

I laid down my head on my books. I was thinking I should ask my aunt Linny to light a candle at St Luke's for the prom. She should light one for me, too, because I was sure I had a brain tumor. A tumor would explain why I agreed to help Nat. It might actually make life easier. If I had a brain tumor, Gilroy couldn't make me serve all those detentions. TJ couldn't bug out on me. It would bum out my brothers, though. Well, not Shawn, but Steven and Billy would miss me when I died. I hoped Ma would pick a coffin that looked like wood, instead of a tacky white one.

Then I realized planning my funeral was sick.

Hector Gonzalez raised his hand and asked the sub for a pass to see Mr Kotlyar, the physics teacher. Hector didn't take physics, but the sub didn't know that, so he wrote the pass. Hector waved to us as he left the room.

One by one, the other kids raised their hands. They needed a pass to see the guidance counsellor about a college essay, or to make up a test they missed last week. Dalinda said she had to see her daughter in the preschool. That was a good one, because Dalinda didn't have any kids, and our school didn't have a preschool. But she got her pass. The stories kept coming, the sub kept smiling and writing out passes. The door opened, closed, opened, closed, and the room got emptier and emptier until it was just me and a couple guys in the back who were dead asleep.

The sub whistled softly and pulled a newspaper out of his briefcase.

And then it hit me.

"You did that on purpose, didn't you?" I asked.

"Excuse me?" he said.

"Letting everybody go. They were all playing you."

"Yep." He unfolded the paper and turned to the page that had the story about Miss Crane's felony theft.

The room was quiet. This guy didn't look so stupid anymore.

"But really, you played them," I said.

He just smiled.

Nat and I were supposed to have a mini-meeting at lunch. Gilroy changed my plans by nabbing me as soon as I stepped into the cafeteria. I had to spend the whole lunch period listening to him blah, blah, blah about "accountability".

If I wanted to be an accountant, I would have taken that class in tenth grade. But I didn't say that.

He said I forced my way on the prom committee just to make him look bad, that I was kissing Banks's butt to spite him. He said he hadn't forgotten who my "so-called boyfriend" was, and he knew the kind of kid I really was. Gilroy was the one who caused TJ to drop out.

I had to laugh. *I* didn't know the kind of kid I was anymore. This guy didn't know me for shit.

He yelled at me when I laughed. Then he blah blahed some more, this time about "respect". A bubble of spit foamed up in the left corner of his mouth. The rest of his mouth was dry and flaky. Didn't he ever hear of ChapStick? Poor Mrs Gilroy, having to kiss those alligator skin lips.

He asked if I had anything to say for myself.

I told him that I was six weeks away from graduation, and I was going to make it no matter how many illegal detentions he threw at me. I told him I had permission from the principal to help my best friend get her prom. And I asked him if I could go, because Nat had scheduled a meeting for me to attend.

That earned me lecture number two on "respect". The bubble of spit grew into a gob. I had better show up for every detention, turn in all homework on time, and keep my nose clean, because he was giving me "no wiggle room, not a damn inch". The gob dripped down his chin, and he wiped it away with his hand.

I promised myself I would never shake that man's hand, not ever.

We never got around to talking about prom security issues.

68.

I missed lunch, but I showed up for all my classes and turned in all my homework that day.

Go, me.

After the last bell, I walked to detention. And who was the day's detention monitor?

Mr New Math Sub.

Go, me!

"You gonna be here the rest of the year?" I asked as he wrote out a pass excusing me.

"As long as they let me stay," he said.

I took the pass. "Anything I can do to help?"

"Get a couple of your friends to complain about me," he said. "That should impress the administration."

I picked up my books. "No problem."

69.

Nat was waiting for me in the hall. It was scary the way that girl could track me down.

"Thank God you got out," she said. "We have so much to do."

"Sorry I missed the lunch meeting. I was talking to Gilroy. How did it go?"

"Short, sweet, and to the point. The gym's a lock and we have a lead on a DJ. I heard you got the English teachers confirmed."

"And the custodians."

"What did Mr Gilroy say?"

"I am disrespectful and have an attitude problem."

"What else is new? Did you guys decide on the security details? Do we have to meet with the police representative?"

"He and I will talk about it tomorrow."

"Good." She pulled out the pink notebook. "We have to call around about renting tables and chairs. We have enough cash for that. We can do it at my house. Grandma is at the Y today. Any chance your family has fifty extra tablecloths we can borrow?"

I held up my hands. "Hold on. I might have to work. I have to call my boss."

"I already did. You're not on tonight."

"You what?"

"I called the restaurant. Two birthday parties cancelled on account of chicken pox, and the manager said he didn't need you."

I leaned against the locker. "You called my boss."

"Yes, and you're off tonight. Everyone is coming to my house to work on the flyers. They have to go up tomorrow or we're screwed. Can we go now?"

I crossed my arms over my chest. "I didn't say you could do that."

"Look, I was just trying to help you," she said. "You were in detention, and you don't have a phone. How were you going to know what to do? I figured I'd be saving you time, making it easier for you. Are you mad?"

"I don't know. I don't think so." I let my arms drop. "Thanks, I think."

"You're welcome, I think. Can we go now?"

"Hang on. Gimme a pen?"

"Why?"

I put my hand out, and she dug out a pen from the bottom of her purse. I started writing in big letters on the track team poster taped to the wall.

"Don't!" she said. "We'll get in trouble."

THE NEW MATH SUB SUCKS!!!!! was what I wrote. I underlined "sucks" and handed back the pen.

"What was all that about?" she asked.

"Insurance."

70.

Nat was a little kid buzzing on birthday cake for the rest of the afternoon. I was the balloon tied to her wrist. She talked to the custodians about using their ladders to put up decorations in the gym, then she talked to Banks about the best time to decorate. We didn't have any decorations yet, but I guess that didn't matter.

Banks said we could use the school's folding chairs and tables. Nat checked it off her list. I told her we would need another committee to scrape the gum off the bottom of the tables. She ignored me.

Monica (weight 141 pounds) met us in the parking lot. She was hard to miss, because of the way she was screaming and jumping up and down like her thong was on fire. She hugged Nat, hugged me, screamed some more, hugged Nat, hugged me. Jumped up and down some more.

Drugs, perhaps?

Hardly. Her uncle who owned a restaurant downtown promised us all the tablecloths we wanted. Monica and Nat jumped up and down and screamed. They hugged.

Everybody agreed to meet at Nat's house to work on flyers.

"You coming, too?" Monica asked.

"Me?" I asked.

"I heard you was moving in with TJ. Somebody heard he bought you a car or a ring or something. Thought you'd be too busy."

"No, um, he's working. Besides I promised Nat. It'll be fun, to um, make flyers."

"That rocks!" screamed Lauren.

She hugged me, and I hugged back, and then we all hugged. I even bounced a little. I was getting better at this committee stuff.

71.

We made flyers at Nat's for hours. Her grandmother came out of the kitchen at dinner time carrying a tray filled with cabbage rolls and tripe for us.

After Nat explained what tripe was, I went to my house to get us some real food.

The Hannigan kitchen was a war zone, and Dad was losing the battle. The window was cracked. There were tools all over the floor and thick dust in the air. Half of the wall behind the table had been ripped out, and Dad was hammering at the half that was still standing.

He didn't hear me come in, because he was singing an old Aerosmith song at the top of his lungs.

I turned off the boom box. "What are you doing?"

Dad stopped in mid-screech and turned around. "Princess! I wondered when you would be home."

"You said you were going to paint. Paint, Dad, not destroy."

He set the hammer on the table. "By the time I got the wallpaper stripped, the wall was a little dinged up. I figured I'd rip it out, put in some new insulation, which we need, throw up new drywall, and paint. It will look good as new. Better."

"It will take you ten years to do this."

He took off his work gloves and brushed the dust out of his beard. "It's a weekend job. Don't be so negative. I've got a buddy helping me."

"I don't see any buddy."

"He's in the john. What are you up to?"

I was rummaging through our cupboards for normal food. "We're having a meeting at Nat's and we're hungry. Does Ma know you're ripping out the kitchen?"

"It was her idea."

I loaded peanut butter, jelly, two cans of olives, a box of Triscuits, and a can of ravioli into an old grocery bag. "So she saw what a crappy job you did with the wallpaper and she flipped."

"She is thrilled she's getting a new kitchen out of this. In fact, she took the boys to stay with her at Linny's to help me out."

"I bet."

The toilet flushed and boots thudded on the stairs. Dad put his gloves back on. "If you're making sandwiches, why don't you slap together a couple for us? That way we can keep working."

I got up on my tiptoes to reach to the very back of the cupboard, where I knew my mother hid her stash of premium chocolate chip macadamia nut cookies.

The boots came down the hall.

"There's still meat loaf in the fridge," I said. "You can split it. So who's helping you? Uncle Danny?"

Found it. A full box. I put the cookies in the bag and looked up at Dad to say good-bye. His helper was standing next to him wearing oversized work boots, a torn Eagles sweatshirt, and jeans slipping off his butt.

"Hey, babe," said TJ.

Ever have one of those moments when you couldn't think of a single thing to say, not even if a guy put a gun to your head and TV cameras were showing the scene live to the whole world, but then when you went to bed that night, you thought of a hundred perfect things you could have said, and you wanted to scream so loud your pillow explodes?

Me standing in our ruined kitchen, looking at TJ holding my Dad's hammer with a moron grin, was one of those moments.

"You bring us dinner?" TJ asked. "Awesome. I'm starved."

I still couldn't think of anything to say. I took the olives out of my bag, put them on the counter, and left.

I slept over at Nat's that night. She talked in her sleep about the price of table favours. I thought about all the smart things I should have said back in my kitchen.

I couldn't sleep, so I went downstairs. Grandma was watching a Spanish-language news show and sewing a hem into Nat's prom gown. I sat down next to her. She put her sewing away in a basket and got a can of ravioli and two forks. We sat and watched the news in Spanish and ate.

Breakfast was homemade blueberry muffins served by Grandma wearing a nightgown and her red bathing cap. The muffins were amazing. I said *"spasibo"* (Russian for "thanks") and took two, then Nat pulled me out the front door.

"How come she bakes all this great stuff for breakfast but cooks animal guts and cabbage for dinner?" I asked.

"Some questions have no answers," Nat said. "Come on. We have to get the posters up before school."

I popped the last bite of muffin in my mouth as we pulled into the parking lot. Monica, Lauren, Junie, and Aisha were waiting for us by the door.

Nat handed out flyers, tape, and muffins, and we split up in three groups. Each group took a floor of the school.

We had an hour.

"What if nobody reads these things?" I asked Nat as I taped a flyer to the door of the boys' locker room.

"Flyers are like old-fashioned Internet news flashes. I'm not worried."

"We really should have made a video. They could play it on cable. Everybody would see it."

Nat ripped off a piece of tape. "You're right. We should have postponed the prom for a year so we could make a video. Why didn't I think of that?" She stuck the tape on the flyer and moved down the hall.

"You don't have to get all sarcastic," I said. "It was just an idea. Where are you going?"

"We're done here. We have to do the band room."

"Don't you want to go inside?"

"Inside where?"

"The locker room, moron. We could stick flyers over the urinals."

"Shut up, that's sick."

"No, not shuttin' up. They need something to look at when they're taking a leak."

76.

By the time the busses started arriving, the flyers were all over the school. Monica high fived me for the urinal idea. Aisha got points for putting the prettiest flyers on the lockers of the coolest girls in school. She made sure that Persia Faulkner had the hippest flyer of all.

Nat was still freaking. "There's so much to do," she said as we walked to health. "A bazillion things."

"We'll get it done," I said.

"How? I'm serious, Ash. We have so many vendors to

cover, phone calls for donations, table favours to make ...
I would kill for a cigarette."

I stopped. "Oh my God. I'm going to die."

"You don't smoke."

"Jonesie will kill me. My tobacco essay? For health?"

"You didn't finish it?"

"I didn't start it."

She grabbed my shoulders. "Ashley Hannigan, this is
a national emergency. If you screw up and get kicked off
my committee I'll take hostages, I swear."

"It's okay, it's okay, calm down. Tell Jonesie I'm puking
in the bathroom. I'll get it done before the end of class."

I wrote the essay in the third-floor bathroom. I wrote
it like I was talking to somebody who needed to screw their
head on straight about cigarettes, somebody like Nat. I
never wrote anything that fast.

Must have been the muffins.

77.

Nat was right about the flyers. People noticed. By lunch,
all you heard about was the prom.

"...in our gym? Here?"

"...still don't have a dress."

"...how much?"

110

"…some phat singer…"

"…he promised…"

"…you goin'?"

"…who's goin'?"

"…it'll be lame…"

"…he'll be so hot…"

"…they'll cancel…"

"…why not?"

Gilroy wasn't stalking me, so I was able to connect with my prom girls sitting at the table by the soda machine. I took the last open seat, next to Lauren. She stole one of my fries.

"Good thing you turned that paper in," Lauren said. "Jonesie was pissed."

"Are you sure she didn't call Gilroy?"

"We distracted her. Got her talking about condoms. Worked like a charm."

Monica pulled the ticket box out of her backpack and clunked it on the table.

"How are sales?" Lauren asked.

"What sales?"

"Everybody's talking about the prom," Lauren said.

"They might be talking, but they ain't buying." Monica

snagged a handful of my fries. "I sold thirteen tickets so far. People are pissed they have to buy another ticket, even if it's only ten bucks."

"They'll be even more pissed if we can't afford the DJ," I said.

"Thirteen?" Lauren asked. "Somebody bought only one ticket?"

"No. Hector bought three. Said he's bringing two dates, because he's 'too much man for one girl'."

We all pretended to vomit.

Monica broke my cookie into three pieces and took two of them. "Maybe this isn't worth it. Why kill ourselves if nobody's going to show up?"

"Excuse me," I said. "Are you off your diet?"

"I didn't have any breakfast." Monica put back one of the cookie pieces. "But you're right. Thanks, Ash."

Nat took the piece of cookie that Monica gave up. "This prom is totally going to work, and everybody is going to show up and have fun." She sipped my chocolate milk and took out her pink notebook. I was starting to hate that thing. "Let's review assignments for this afternoon."

Everybody groaned. The excuses flew. Lauren had to tutor a second grader. Junie had to babysit her cousin. Aisha had to work at BK right after school and the shoe store at six. Monica was leaving at the end of eighth period to visit her sister in Delaware for the weekend.

Every time a girl lied her way out of the afternoon's

work, Nat drew a frowny face next to her name in the pink notebook.

I chewed my tiny piece of cookie. If everybody bailed, I'd be off the hook, too. I could spend the weekend at Aunt Linny's. No, wait. My brothers were there. I had lots of relatives, somebody would let me crash for the weekend. I could sleep, work, sleep some more. Maybe TJ could finally take me to see the apartment. I was starting to get excited about it in a stomach ache kind of way. Ma was going to flip out when she heard, but then she'd get excited, too, and we could go to Penney's and buy curtains.

The bell rang, and the other girls shot out of there, like the lazy cowards they were. Nat drew a smiley face next to her own name and another one next to mine.

"Looks like it'll just be the two of us," she said. "You have to get out of detention early again. We have a lot of begging to do this afternoon."

78.

When she said "begging", she meant that we had to shake down the stores around the school.

Nat said it nicer as we walked out of school. "We're going to solicit the merchants on Bonventura Street for donations and supplies."

"Soliciting means turning tricks, you know," I said.

"You're making that up."

"No, really. If we were whores, we could get all kinds of donations."

"Not funny."

"It's kind of funny. Where do we start?"

In Nat's fantasy world we'd step into a store, introduce ourselves to the manager, explain why we were "seeking a donation" and walk out with an armful of loot.

Here's how it worked in reality.

We'd press a buzzer to get the door unlocked. When we were in the store, the owner looked us over to see if we were the kind of innocent-looking girls who hide handguns in their bras. In a back room, a dog growled. The owner would ask what we wanted. Nat read from her index card, and the owner would say, "Cut to the chase, hon, whattyouwan?" Nat would get all red in the face, and I would ask for something from our list: napkins, plastic cups, decorations, soda, cookies, lights, streamers, confetti, or the loan of a video camera. They could give us cash, too.

When the owners stopped laughing, the answer was always the same: "Ugottabeouttayourfreakinmind."

79.

We hit seventeen stores and scored a big fat nothing.

Getting turned down makes you hungry. I bought us a

soft pretzel and a Diet Coke to split, and we sat on a kerb. A group of girls were playing double Dutch in the parking lot across the street.

Nat licked the salt off her half of the pretzel. "This is harder than I thought."

I spread mustard on my half. "Maybe we could decorate the gym with toilet paper."

"You can make lots of things out of toilet paper," she said. "I've read articles."

"You're scaring me, Shulmensky."

The double-Dutch girls twirled their ropes and sang, "Down, down, baby, down by the roller coaster, sweet, sweet baby, I'm never let you go..."

Nat put a grain of salt on her tongue. "What if Monica was right? What if we can't pull it off?"

One of the jumpers got tangled in the ropes, and they all burst out in giggles.

"Hmm." If we couldn't pull it off, I'd dance in the street. Couldn't say that, though.

Nat sipped the Coke. "I mean, look at us. We're begging for paper napkins and getting squat."

The girls across the street untangled their ropes and started again. "Down, down, baby, down by the roller coaster..."

I swallowed. "Maybe we're doing this bass-ackwards, starting with these little stores."

"Like we have a choice."

"You want money, you gonna ask a poor person? Hell, no. You ask a rich person."

"Do you know any rich people?"

"Of course not. But I know where they shop."

"What, you want us to go to King of Prussia or something?"

King of Prussia was this mega-mother-blinging mall, the Disneyland of shopping for the rich people who live around Philly. You could fit our whole house in one of the elevators. The floors are made out of marble, the ceilings have stained glass, and the escalators are polished three times a day. Even the bathrooms smell good, like the people who shop there never do anything smelly, if you know what I mean.

I licked the mustard off my fingers. "Exactly. We could go tomorrow."

Before she could say anything else, Nat's cell rang. "Hello? This is Natalia. Yes. Yes, sir."

I took the last bite of my pretzel. Across the street, the shortest girl did a cartwheel and bounced up perfectly between the swinging ropes.

"I'm on my way. Thank you for calling." Nat closed her phone, stood up, and brushed the salt off her legs.

"What's going on?" I asked.

"My grandmother is in a church down at Broad and Logan."

"So? Grandma Hannigan spends half her life in a church."

"My grandmother is *Jewish*."

"Oh. And she's not at a Jewish church, is she?"

"It's called a synagogue, dumbass. And no, she's not there. She's at Holy Hands AME."

"So what's the problem?"

"It sounds like she's in their dunk tank."

"They have a dunk tank?"

"It's a special pool, the minister said."

"For baptizing?"

"Whatever. It's a Christian thing. All you guys do it."

"Catholics don't dunk. We dab. But wait, your grandma went swimming in the baptismal pool?"

"Wrong. She is *still* swimming in the baptismal pool. She won't get out."

80.

It took us twenty minutes to find the church, and another five to find a parking place and walk back to the church. Reverend Pinkney was waiting for us at the door.

I don't know what Nat said to her grandmother, but it did not sound polite. Grandma muttered, but she finally took Nat's hand and climbed out of the little pool and dried off.

Reverend Pinkney offered to pray for us. Nat told him that was very kind and helped Grandma down the steps. I pulled him aside and gave him my list. We needed prayers for Nat's grandmother (obviously), for our prom, for me graduating, and for my parents, who needed all the help they could get.

"Is that everything?" Reverend Pinkney asked.

"Why don't you throw in an extra one for me, just general-like. You know, to make sure all the bases are covered. I'm stressing a little these days. Thanks."

81.

I made bologna sandwiches at the Shulmenskys' while Nat took Grandma upstairs to change. I set the table nice and laid the sandwiches on plates with potato chips and homemade pickles I found in the fridge.

Grandma came downstairs wearing a long red skirt I never saw before. Nat led her to the table, and she sat down without any fuss. I wolfed down my sandwich. Nat tore her crust into little pieces. Grandma nodded and jabbered at me; then she started singing.

"She's happy because she got to go swimming," Nat explained.

"Can't blame her for that," I said.

The kitchen door opened, and Nat's father came in. Mr Shulmensky always reminded me of a bald snowman with glasses – round head, round belly, big round butt, and a friendly smile that always made me feel better. He put his newspaper on the counter. "Well, hello, Ashley. Good to see you at our table. How are your parents? Baby come yet?"

Nat cut in and told her dad about the dunk tank. He stopped smiling and switched into Russian. Grandma took her pickle into the living room. Nat and Mr Shulmensky followed her. The Russian got loud.

I cleared the dirty dishes off the table and loaded them into the dishwasher. When Nat started to cry, I went home.

82.

I knew our kitchen would still be a wreck. Dad's projects took months, sometimes years. We'd be living with torn-out walls, tools on the floor, and dust for months. Ma would spend the next six months complaining, and Dad would finish the job in time to call it her Christmas present.

That's why I was so confused when I opened the back door.

The walls were done ... perfectly finished and painted margarine yellow. The floor was mopped, the counters wiped down, and there weren't any tools in sight. The chairs stood neatly around the table. There was a vase of daffodils – real flowers – in the middle of the table.

I reached for the door. I was in the wrong house.

"Is that you, princess?"

Dad walked in, toweling his hair dry. He was wearing clean jeans and a shirt with buttons down the front. He had trimmed his beard and was grinning like a pirate. "Looks pretty good, don't it?"

I had to sit down. "What happened?"

He threw the towel down the steps to the basement and combed his fingers through his hair. "What do you mean? We finished. Not a big deal, is it?"

"You're going to hurt yourself, you keep smiling like that."

"You should have seen your mother's face." He shook his head and chuckled. "Priceless."

"No offence, Dad, but how did you do it? I mean, it took you a month to put up the shelf in the bathroom."

He leaned against the counter and crossed his arms. "Truth? It was TJ."

"TJ? My TJ?"

"Yep. He got his cousins from Jersey to help. They do a lot of construction around Cherry Hill. You shoulda seen them, Ash. Those guys just flew."

"My TJ?"

"Yeah, maybe you should have been nicer to him. I'm telling you, Ash, he really came through for us. And he has a big night planned for you two tomorrow. Said he'd pick you up around six."

"My TJ helped with this?"

"Couldn't have done it without him. He left that card for you on the table. A real romantic, isn't he?"

I ripped open the envelope. It was a mushy card, with a picture of two little kids holding hands on the front. Inside, TJ had drawn a heart with our initials in it: "TJB + AMH 4eva."

I could feel the mad in me leaking out like water between my fingers. *Damn.*

Dad chuckled again. "I'm out of here, kiddo. Got a hot date with your mother."

"Do I have to babysit the boys?"

"Nope, they're staying at Linny's again. You going out?"

"I'm going to sleep. I'm beat. This prom stuff is wiping me out."

He winked. "We'll try not to wake you when we get home. Gonna be a great night!"

"Ew, don't say that. Parents should not have sex. You two are disgusting perverts."

"Yeah, I know. Ain't it great?"

83.

The next morning, I woke up to the smell of perfume and the sound of a flock of crows. I rolled over. Perfume and crows, must be a nightmare.

Perfume. Crows. Ma was home.

A woman giggled. It sounded like a poodle with hiccups.

Ma was home and she had Aunt Linny with her.

Another laugh. This one sounded like a live chicken being shoved in a blender.

Aunt Joan.

And then a laugh that turned into a hacking cough.

Aunt Sharon.

I groaned and pulled the pillow over my head. They were all here.

A herd of screaming buffalo pounded up the stairs and burst into my room. Billy jumped on my bed. "Wake up, wake up!"

Steven followed him. "Ma says you have to get dressed."

Billy climbed on my rear and bounced. "Get up, big butt."

"TJ's called three times already," Steven said. "You have to go out with him tonight."

"Get up, big butt. The aunts brought—"

Steven covered Billy's mouth with his hand. "There's a surprise for you downstairs. You better hurry before Ma explodes."

Downstairs, Aunt Linny giggled.

My mother and her three sisters were waiting for me in the living room, like something out of a sick fairy tale. Ma was plopped in the middle of the couch with a box of chocolate doughnuts on her belly. Aunt Linny was on her left, and Aunt Sharon was on her right, closest to the door. Aunt Joan filled the recliner.

The four of them screamed when they saw me. Aunt Sharon jumped up and gave me a hug, rocking side to side. "We are so excited!" Rock, rock, rock. "This is gonna be great!" Rock, rock, rock.

Ma waved a doughnut at us. "Let her go, Shar. You'll make her seasick."

Aunt Sharon turned me loose, and I stumbled over a pile of dress shoes. That was weird. We never had dress shoes in the living room before. I blinked and looked around the room. The coffee table was hidden under a huge heap of dresses, and the entertainment centre was covered by hanging garment bags.

"What's going on?" I asked.

"My baby is going to the prom," Ma said.

She knew.

Aunt Linny pulled a hideous green dress off the table. "The prom," she sighed. "Oh, Ashley..." She petted the dress. "The prom is everything." She bit her lip and blinked hard. "Just everything."

"No waterworks," Aunt Sharon warned. "You promised."

If I walked over to Bonventura, I could join the army. Better yet, if I called the recruiter and invited him over to meet my family, I bet he'd give me a signing bonus because he'd feel so bad for me.

Aunt Sharon leaned forward to put out her cigarette. "This is going to be the best night of your life, Ash, swear to God. I can remember every minute of my prom."

No, I shouldn't walk. I should run screaming all the way to the recruiting office and beg the army to take me.

Aunt Joan lit two cigarettes and handed one to Aunt Sharon. "You're going with TJ, right? This is going to be so freaking romantic. Is he going to wear a tux? He should get one of them tall hats, you know?"

Of course, with my luck, I'd get assigned to something like sweeping minefields. But I'd take it. I'd volunteer, even.

"You should have seen your mother's face when she found out," Aunt Sharon said. "She didn't know if she should be pissed off or overjoyed."

That comment hit a nerve. "How did you find out? Wait a minute..." I whirled around. "Steven!"

A voice answered from the kitchen. "It wasn't me!"

"Relax, peanut," Ma said. "It wasn't your brothers. Your father told me the news. Last night."

"Bless his heart," said Aunt Joan.

"Bless his heart," echoed Aunt Sharon.

"You shoulda heard her," added Aunt Linny. "As soon as she finds out: 'Ash needs a dress. Omigod, Ash needs a dress. Thank you, Jesus, she needs a dress.'"

"Linny called us right away," Aunt Joan said. "We rounded up all the prom dresses we could."

"Bridesmaid dresses, too," added Aunt Sharon. "And shoes. And my friend Carmen has a closet of purses, oh my God, you should see it."

"Where is Dad?" I asked. "I need to kill him."

Aunt Linny petted the green dress again. "The hardware store. He's on a roll, he said. Wants to finish the basement for you. When he's not being an asshole, your father is a truly wonderful human being."

Aunt Joan reached for another doughnut. "He told my Joe that he's got your ride all lined up. Slick, he said."

"Enough yakking," Ma said. "Sharon, pull the blinds. Ashley, try these on. You can change in the dining room."

"But Maaa," I whined.

Four sets of steely blue eyes pinned me up against the wall.

85.

Somewhere in America there was a girl who had nobody. No mother getting buzzed on chocolate doughnuts and secondhand smoke. No aunts who kept their prom dresses twenty years too long. No relatives or friends of relatives or neighbours of relatives who heard that the girl was going to a prom and had a sister whose daughter went last year and I'm sure we could borrow the gown, because you never know, it could fit.

I hoped that girl knew how lucky she was.

86.

The first dress I was handed came from somebody named Stacey Wiggans, whose mother worked with Aunt Joan. I never met Stacey Wiggans, but I'll know her if I see her on the street. She has boobs the size of Alaska.

I zipped it up and stepped into the living room. Ma took one look and said, "I can see all the way to your belly button. Take it off."

Aunt Linny handed me something black and velvet. "Try this."

"Black is for funerals," I said.

"Black is sophisticated; don't argue."

I took off the Stacey Wiggans Big Boob Special and shimmied into the black dress.

"Ta-da!"

Aunt Joan snorted smoke out her nose. Ma cracked up. "Okay, sophisticated you're not. Next."

Next was a blue polka-dot disaster, then came something that looked like a bedspread, then a gold shimmery thing that wouldn't go over my hips, and then a dark purple beaded strapless that was pretty except that it fell down every time I raised my arms.

"Again with the boobs," sighed Aunt Sharon.

A black dress with white stripes around the hem made me look like a lounge singer. The brown and gold thing made me look like a stripper. The pink one that came with matching gloves reminded me too much of a confirmation dress. There were two skintight dresses that looked like mermaid costumes, without the tails. I refused to touch Aunt Joan's collection from the seventies. You looked at the dresses and you thought "bonfire."

Ma unzipped a garment bag. "This one," she said. "The colour is right for you."

She was right. It was a soft shade of dark green, the colour of the leaves in the park when the sun is going down. The fabric was lightweight velvet. I stepped into it and held my breath as I worked it up over my thighs (should not have eaten ice cream for the last month) and my butt (too much pizza). It was tight, sexy tight.

"Turn around," Ma said. "Let me zip you."

I pushed all the air out of my lungs and pretended I had a twenty-three-inch waist.

Ma zipped. "Suck it in."

"It is sucked in."

She pulled the zipper up a little farther.

"Smush your ribs together."

"What?"

She grunted and zipped me all the way up.

"It's a little tight," I squeaked.

"You'll lose weight," Ma said. "Turn around."

"Oooooooh," said the aunts.

"This is definitely the one, honey," Ma said.

I looked down. The dress fit like green velvet skin. I had a waist and hips and boobs, and it didn't show the fat on the tops of my thighs that I hate more than anything, even my freckles.

"Oooooooooh," said the aunts again.

Ma checked me out head to toe. "You might need a different date."

"Why?" I asked.

"TJ Barnes is not good enough for that dress. You need George Clooney."

"That's sick. He's older than Dad."

"You know what I mean. Twirl around."

I stepped over the shoe pile and – *rii-iiii-iiip.*

The aunts gasped.

"Oh, well," Ma said. "Easy come, easy go."

"Give it here," Aunt Linny said. "I'll fix it."

Ma unzipped me and studied the tear. "It's hopeless, Lynn. It's not a seam, the fabric tore across her ass. Take a look." She handed it to Aunt Linny, who sighed. The perfect green dress was dead.

Ma pointed to a pink bridesmaid's dress. "That one has a stain, but we can get it out."

I dragged the pink thing into the dining room and pulled it on. "I'm done after this, Ma."

"Yeah, yeah, yeah, whatever. Show me the dress."

I inhaled so I could pull the zipper to the top and stepped into the archway.

"You have a very unusual figure, know that?" Aunt Sharon said. "I never noticed that before."

Aunt Linny squinted at me. "She's built like her father's family."

"How many days till this prom again?" Aunt Joan asked.

"Six," I said.

Aunt Sharon finished her doughnut. "You're screwed, honey."

87.

There was a knock on the front door. It opened and Nat stuck in her head. "Hey. You ready?"

"Natalia, come in!" Ma said. "You remember my sisters."

Nat stepped in, her grandmother close behind. "Hello, everyone."

129

The aunts said their hellos and nodded at Grandma.

"You look busy," Nat said.

"We're finding her a prom dress," Aunt Joan said.

"Don't laugh," I warned.

"And shoes," added Aunt Linny. "You got to have the right shoes."

"I am not trying on other people's shoes," I said. "That is too nasty to think about."

Nat eyed the shoe pile. "You got any fives in there?"

"Be my guest," Aunt Joan said.

While Nat pawed through the shoes, Grandma squeezed between Ma and Aunt Linny on the couch. Grandma leaned over and stared at the rip Aunt Linny was trying to fix. She muttered, snagged the sewing out of Aunt Linny's hands, and tore out the stitches with her teeth.

"Hey," Aunt Linny said.

"Leave her alone," said Ma. "It's easier that way."

Nat held up a pair of silver stilettos. "I like these. Is that the dress you're gonna wear, Ash?"

I pulled down the zipper. "Shut up."

"You should see her in that one." Aunt Joan pointed to the bedspread dress hanging off the entertainment centre. "She looked like a vision."

I stripped off the pink thing. "A vision you get after a night of Jell-O shots."

"What do you know about Jell-O shots?" Aunt Joan asked.

130

"Nothing," Ma said. "If she knows what's good for her, she knows nothing. Put on another dress, honey."

"That was the last one."

"What?"

"I tried them all on, Ma, I'm done. Show's over."

"I'll call my friend Marnie. She has a huge closet."

"No, you won't. I don't need a dress. I'll wear my black skirt or khakis."

"Anything but khakis." Nat inspected the heel on a pair of red open-toe sandals. "How much does it cost to dye shoes?"

"Who dyes shoes?" I asked. "I'll wear my black skirt and I'll help, but you're wasting your time trying to find me a dress."

Grandma handed the green velvet dress back to Aunt Linny.

"Will you look at this," Aunt Linny said, holding the repaired rip up to the light. "She's good."

Nat buckled the red sandals on her feet and stood up. "She was a seamstress in Russia."

"She was famous," Ma said. "Got sent to jail."

"They sent her to jail for her sewing?" Aunt Linny asked. "And I thought Republicans were tough. Watch it, honey. You could hurt yourself on those things."

Nat teetered dangerously on the high heels and grabbed for the back of the recliner. "She was in prison because of politics."

"That sounds like the Republicans," Aunt Linny said.

"Don't start," Aunt Joan said. "The Democrats are no better."

I pulled on my shorts. "We gotta go. Nat and me are going to the mall."

Nat wobbled from the recliner to the couch. "Grandma's coming, too."

"What do you need at the mall?" Ma asked.

"Prom donations," I said.

"Like what?"

"Decorations, lights, tablecloths, favours." I put on my shirt. "Pretty much anything that will make it feel like it's not a middle school dance."

"So where are you going?"

"King of Prussia."

"*That's* what *I'm* talking about!" Aunt Joan pulled up the handle of the recliner and her feet dropped to the floor with a thud. "I'm going with you."

Aunt Linny squealed. "Me, too."

"Fuggettaboutit," I said.

"What are you, nuts?" Aunt Sharon asked. "We are the Queens of Free. Between us we got, like, sixty years on PTA committees. You're a kid, what do you know?"

"We're going, and that's that." Ma tried to reach her feet, but leaned back against the couch. "Would one of youse please tie my sneakers? And take off those damn heels before you hurt yourself, Natalia."

"This is a bad idea, Nat."

"This was your idea, Ash."

"No, going to the mall was my idea. Bringing my family and Grandma – I had nothing to do with that."

"So what do you want me to do, turn the car around? Look, your aunt is getting ready to pass me, and I'm doing seventy."

"That's my mother driving."

"How can she reach the steering wheel?"

"Dad says her arms get longer with each pregnancy."

"That's kind of creepy."

"Shut up and drive, Nat."

"Shuttin' up."

Ma took charge when we met up at the mall. She split us up into three groups: Aunts Linny and Sharon, Aunt Joan with Nat and Grandma, and Ma and me. Group one was in charge of decorations for the walls and group two was in charge of decorations for the tables.

Ma took my arm as we walked away. "What are we in charge of?" I asked.

"You'll see," she said. "This looks good. Let's start here."

"No, let's not. This is a dress store, Ma. We need party favours. Balloons. There's nothing here for us."

We went in.

The ladies behind the counter stared as Ma stopped in front of a rack of long dresses.

"We can't afford this," I whispered.

"You have a very limited imagination, Ashley." She rubbed a grey silk sleeve between her fingers. "Creativity, that's what you need."

I pointed to the red-hot price tag. "Money, that's what I need. You don't make this much in a whole month. We're wasting our time."

"Ooooh!" Ma clutched the display rack.

"What?"

She dropped her purse and reached for her belly.

"Is she all right?" asked the saleswoman.

"Don't you dare," I hissed.

Ma turned to the woman. "It's nothing, it's nothing. Could you get me a chair, please? No, ah, not there. Could you move it closer to the dressing room? Great, thanks. Is there any chance you could get me some water? Or a soda?"

The saleswomen ran around like squirrels, trying to do anything that would keep my mother from giving birth in the middle of the store. They sat her down in a fancy chair that looked like it came from a museum, and poured her a glass of lemonade. The "contractions" stopped and Ma started bullshitting the ladies about being pregnant with twins.

"She's fine," I said. "She's not due for another month."

A little bell rang as more customers walked in. "Go on, dears, I'll be fine. I know you have your work to do. I'll sit for a few more minutes, just to be sure. Since we're here, Ashley, honey, why don't you try on a few dresses?"

"Ma."

"Oh, go on."

"Maaa."

"You wouldn't want me to have any more nasty contractions now, would you?"

She winked at me.

I grabbed the grey silk dress in my size.

90.

It took the whole afternoon, four stores, and three episodes of "early labour" with the "twins," but Ma finally got what she wanted. When we met up with the others at the food court, we were carrying a bag. Inside the bag was a dress. It was a prom dress. It was pink. It was originally seventy per cent off, but Ma got it down to eighty-five per cent off by screaming, "My water broke!" while we were checking out.

The aunts and Nat loved my dress. They oohhed and aahed and said all the things you'd think, only they said it so loud the security guard who was keeping the food court safe wandered over to see what the commotion was about.

Grandma Shulmensky hated the dress. When Ma pulled it out of the bag, she spat on the marble floor, a big wet one. The guard said something into his radio and Nat said something that did not sound polite in Russian. Grandma spat a second time.

"Okay, then, time for us to hit the road," said Aunt Sharon. "She is a feisty one, ain't she?"

We hustled Grandma out to the parking lot, with two security guards tagging behind us until we were outside.

The aunts showed us their loot when we got to the cars. The kitchen store gave Nat and Aunt Joan a bag full of paper napkins that were too wrinkled to sell and the bookstore gave them gift certificates for door prizes.

Aunt Linny said, "Ha! We did way better."

Aunt Joan lit a cigarette. "Sure you did."

"We got Christmas lights." She shook a huge department store bag.

Aunt Joan put her lighter away. "Aren't you a little old for shoplifting, Linny?"

"They really gave them to us," Aunt Sharon said.

Ma looked in the bag. "You've got hundreds of dollars of Christmas lights in here!"

"Why did they give them to you?" Aunt Joan asked.

Aunt Sharon unlocked her car. "Because we helped this really sweet gal in luggage who had a pig for a floor manager, and then we got to talking with her because Ashley's graduating and needs a job and maybe they're hiring. I got you applications for five stores, Ash, you'll make a killing with the employee discounts. Anywho, the luggage gal tells us about these Christmas decorations that were never returned to the main warehouse and now they're taking up a shelf in the back room. Next thing you know we were in the office, a few phone calls were made, and we wound up with the lights." She opened the door. "When you fill out the application, put down that Patty recommended you, Ash. You could do worse than a steady job in luggage."

92.

Oh. The other thing that happened at the mall was that Grandma stole a container of chai latte gelato. It's expensive, beige ice cream.

She kept it in her purse until we got home.

I helped Nat clean the car.

That night, we sat down like a normal family for dinner: pork chops, baked potatoes, salad, applesauce, and something in a covered casserole dish.

Dad passed the dish to me. "Try the beans. It's your grandmother's recipe. Has bacon in it."

I shook my head. "Don't suck up to me with beans. I'm not talking to you."

"What? What did I do now?"

"You told the whole world about the prom thing, that's what you did."

"Get over yourself, Ashley, and take some beans," Ma said. "Wait until you see her in this dress, George. You'll die."

I put two beans on my plate. "Well, he's not dying tonight because I refuse to put that thing on."

"Yeah, yeah, yeah." Ma cut up Billy's pork chop. "And you should have seen the Christmas lights that Sharon got. I don't know how she does it, I swear."

My chop had the consistency of a purse. I drowned it in ketchup and chewed until my teeth hurt, then I fed the rest of it, piece by piece, to Mutt, lying at my feet.

Ma was centre stage, telling Dad about the mall and the shopping, and how she got that last fifteen per cent off my dress. Steven and Shawn made bean jokes. Billy mixed ketchup into his applesauce and poured it over his potato, then said he wasn't hungry, which made Ma yell. By the time I cleared the table, I had a headache that started near my belly button and looped around my neck like a noose.

"I'm going to lie down," I said.

"You can't do that," Ma said. She drank some milk from Billy's glass. "You're gonna try on that dress. I want to see the hem; we might want to take it up a little. Plus we have to find a bra that won't show."

"I wanna play Spider-Man," Billy said.

"No more Spider-Man." Steven helped me scrape the plates. "We'll play kickball. You can be on my team, Ash."

"No fair," said Shawn. "She can kick it downtown. If you get Ash, you gotta take Billy."

"Hold it, hold it, time out!" Dad said. "Ashley spent the whole day with your aunts, boys; she deserves a break."

"What are you saying about my sisters?" Ma asked.

"Nothing, sweetness. I just think Ashley should chill. She can watch the game with me. Wouldn't that be fun, princess? The Phillies are going to crush the Yankees."

I stacked the plates in the sink. "I'm not talking to you."

"She's not talking to you," Ma said. "Ha. Why don't you invite Natalia over so she can see you in your dress? She could bring hers, too. We'll make it a little party, a girly night."

My headache exploded like fireworks into every strand

of my hair. Families should come with volume buttons. Better yet, a mute button. That's what I needed: a mute button, three Tylenol, and a soft pillow.

Instead, I got TJ.

He knocked on the back door and walked in with a shy grin, shook Dad's hand, let Ma kiss his cheek, turned down dinner because he already ate. His shirt was ironed, and his sneakers were tied, and I could smell his cologne from where I was sitting. My heart started beating faster even though I told it not to. Even though he wasn't touching me, I could feel his hands sliding around my waist. My heart pounded.

"You ready to go?" he asked.

My options were what you call limited: a night with the inmates in the insane asylum, arguing about dresses and shoes and why the Phillies won't spend money on their pitching staff, or a night with TJ.

"We riding in a bus again?"

"I borrowed the El Camino," he said. "The night is ours."

94.

I buckled my seat belt, rolled down the window and leaned against the door. TJ started up the car and pulled away from the kerb.

"You're a dog," I said. "I'm still pissed, you know. You

think you can stand me up whenever you want, then you suck up to my dad to get back in good with me."

"All true," he said. "I'm sorry."

"You're disrespectful, sneaky, and you're always late."

"Also true." TJ switched on the CD player. It was cued up to one of my favourite songs, a slow, hot love song. "I'm very sorry."

"The only reason you helped Dad was to get back with me."

TJ braked for a red light. "Yep. I'm sorry."

And then he didn't say anything. When the light turned green, he drove the speed limit. When the song ended, he skipped the next two tracks to another one of my favourites. At the next red light he said, "I'm sorry, Ash." At the light after that, he said, "I am really, truly sorry I pissed you off."

"Are you going to apologize every time we stop at a red light?"

"Women like apologies, your dad said."

"He did?"

"He told me all kinds of stuff about women."

"Oh, man."

"So I am officially, one hundred per cent sorry I pissed you off, my darling, beautiful Ashley."

We had fifteen more red lights so I listened to fifteen more apologies before we pulled into Sam's Best Hoagies. I got an Italian with extra peppers and no onions. TJ got a foot-long cheesesteak, no onions, out of respect for me. We ate in the car because he had scored a couple mini bottles of raspberry vodka, and hoagie shops don't want you pounding vodka at their tables.

The apologies put me in a better mood. The vodka didn't hurt. By the time we were done eating, we felt normal again, talking and touching and throwing stuff at each other. TJ told me about working with his cousin and going after a job at the loading dock of Wal-Mart. I told him about Gilroy treating me like dirt and Nat's grandmother swimming at the Baptist church and my dress and the prom stuff.

"Ma says you gotta get a tux," I said.

"Aw, Ash, I don't want a monkey suit. I'll look like a dork."

"They're stuffing me into a dress, so you gotta have a tux." I sucked olive oil off my thumb. "Unless you want me to go with some other guy."

"He'd be a dead guy. I'll get a tux. I don't know about a limo. We're talking big bucks, Ash."

"Don't worry. Dad said he'd take care of that."

TJ rolled his cheesesteak wrapper into a ball and tossed it in the backseat. "We really have to go? You're sure."

"Yes, we do. Quit bitching."

He burped and started the car. "What time is it?"

"I don't know. Eight? Quarter after?"

"Cool. We can go then."

"To the apartment?"

"Prepare yourself, gorgeous."

95.

"You're gonna love it, you're gonna love it, you're gonna love it. No, don't open your eyes yet, couple more steps, no, you don't want to touch that. Hang on. Don't move."

I stood with my eyes squeezed shut while TJ did something with a handful of keys. We were in a hallway at the top of a staircase that smelled like the front steps of the homeless shelter. It also smelled like oil, or maybe gas. TJ led me inside.

"Okay. Now you can look."

I opened my eyes.

"It's ours," he said. "All ours, yours and mine, Ash. Can you believe it?"

The apartment was as big as my living room. The left-hand wall was stacked with shelves full of greasy engine parts and tools. A grey garbage can stood in front of the shelves, a broom leaning up against it. To the right of the door there was a small table with a microwave and two plastic chairs. Three grocery bags were lined up next to the table.

Dead ahead, against the far wall I saw a skinny

mattress covered with a red blanket. It had two pillows. There were cardboard boxes stacked near to the bed with an old TV on the top. In the far back corner, a shower curtain hung down from the ceiling.

"This is it?"

"All ours. Awesome, huh? What do you think?"

"Um, what's behind the curtain?"

"The toilet. Marty's gonna put in a full bathroom this fall. Until then I figured we could shower at your parents' or at Aunt Lana's. What do you think?"

I thought an apartment was supposed to have rooms. And walls. And at least one closet. I thought my first apartment would have a sunny kitchen and a bathroom with a tub, and it would be in a building with an exercise room on the first floor and maybe a doorman.

"It's, um, you've worked hard."

"It rocks, doesn't it? Look here." TJ reached in a grocery bag and pulled out a box of microwave popcorn. "I got our first groceries." He opened the box and started a bag of popcorn in the microwave. "The next thing we need is a refrigerator. And then a little stove or something so we can cook steaks. You can come in, you know. This is all yours. Yours and mine."

I closed the door behind me.

"We own those tools? And that muffler?"

"No, dummy. They belong to Marty's garage downstairs. Marty, he owns this place, he's charging us half price if we let him store stuff up here. Plus we pay a flat fifty bucks for heat and electric. It don't get no better than that."

"We're living above a garage."

"For a little while. We'll move to a bigger place once we save up enough."

"But what about when they're working downstairs? Won't it be noisy?"

"I figure we'll be at work, too, so what's the difference?"

My foot bumped against something and I looked down. "That's, um, a pretty rug."

"Aunt Lana gave it to us. A housewarming present, she said."

"The floor is clean."

"I been busting my ass getting it ready." The microwave beeped. TJ took out the popcorn and grabbed a bottle of Gatorade from the grocery bag. "Our first meal. Let's get comfortable. You want soda instead? There's a bodega down the corner."

"No. This is okay."

He took my hand and walked me to the bed. "I knew you'd like it. Wanna watch the game? The Yankees suck, I bet we're up by six."

He sat down. I sat down. The popcorn sat between us. I ate popcorn and watched the Yankees beat the crap out of the Phillies.

TJ talked nonstop for four innings. He was full of ideas, like how maybe he shouldn't take the Wal-Mart job because they didn't have a union and we needed benefits, and how I should go full-time at EZ-CHEEZ-E and start sucking up to get the hostess job, or at least tell the boss I needed overtime, or I could get a second job, maybe Aunt Lana could get me in at The Haystack. He knew a place we could rent furniture for cheap. He knew a guy who could set us up with a full-sized refrigerator. By September he figured we could get a couple credit cards and pick up a plasma TV, a laptop, and all the video games we wanted.

TJ had so many things to say that he only ate one handful of popcorn. I ate the rest so I didn't have to talk. The plasma TV sounded good. I always looked at those when I went into Best Buy. If we got a good game system to hook up to it, my brothers would be blown away. I wasn't so pumped about working full-time at the restaurant or picking up hours in a bar. I mean, I wasn't going to be a doctor or nothing, but there were other jobs out there, like office assistant or running the deli counter at Giant or mall security. But I was too buzzed to start an argument, and besides that's when he took my present out of the last grocery bag.

A cell phone.

"We're on a family plan, you and me," TJ said. "This proves once and for all that I love you. Sometimes you forget that, you know."

My own cell phone! I was, like, the only person in my school who didn't have one.

I kissed him and cuddled up against him, and the baseball game was boring, and he was feeling like a man, and I was feeling lonely, so we got out of our clothes and under the covers.

96.

He was snoring when I left. I caught the bus at the corner and sat right behind the driver. It took two transfers and an hour to get home.

My parents were sleeping on the couch when I got in, curled up against each other, with Ma's head on Dad's chest and his fingers tangled in her hair. Photo albums lay open out on the table next to a bottle of Tums. Dad's stomach probably acted up after the Yankees scored four runs in the fifth.

A responsible kid would have woken them up and sent them to bed. Ma's back was going to kill her in the morning, and Dad's heartburn would bug him all day. But they looked so cute in an old people way, I couldn't do it.

I brought down the comforter from their bed and covered them with it.

I overslept. Bad move when you're scheduled for a double shift.

Ma was just making coffee when I ran into the kitchen. Dad was snoring like a dying rhino on the couch. When I realized that Dad's snores sounded just like TJ's snores, I tripped over the laundry piled up by the basement door.

"Watch yourself," Ma said. "You almost broke your neck. What's the hurry?"

I poured a glass of orange juice and gulped it. "Late for work. Isn't he ever going to fix the dryer?"

"Don't know why you care," Ma said. "Don't see you volunteering to go to the laundromat."

"It's just a question. I get off at nine tonight."

"Gimme a kiss, I didn't mean to bitch at you."

I let her hug me and plant a morning breath kiss on my cheek.

"You have a good time last night?"

"It was okay. We got hoagies. Hung out."

"Why can't you hang out here? You two could play cards with us or something."

"Whatever. I'll ask him. If Nat calls, tell her I'm at work."

"Wait, you need some toast and butter."

"I don't have time for toast."

"Here." She handed me an apple from the bowl by the sink. "You need to eat better."

I took the apple. "Gotta go."

"Don't put up with any crap," she called after me.

Work was insanely busy from the second we opened. The lunch shift flew by so fast I didn't have time to enjoy a ten-dollar tip given to me by a mom whose kids chewed with their mouths closed and said thank you. I wasn't sure they were human.

Lunch melted into the early dinner crowd without a break. It was so crazy I didn't have a second to think about TJ and the way "our" place smelled or the fact that the toilet was in the corner behind a shower curtain. If my life could have been that busy 24/7, everything would have been way easier.

The early dinner crowd turned into the regular dinner crowd. My back hurt and my tail dragged. One of the cooks had a fight with a dishwasher. They beat each other up by the Dumpster, and the dishwasher lost two teeth. The manager should have fired both of them, but good cooks are hard to find, so he fired the dishwasher and told the cook to wash his hands and get back to work.

The regular dinner turned into late dinner. Overtired

kids had temper tantrums in the aisles, the boys on the arcade games were getting vicious, and parents kept looking at their watches. My tips shrank and my tail felt like it was filled with lead. I wanted to go home, but not to my house/home because then I'd have to deal with my family, and I didn't want to go to the slimy apartment/ home because it was filled with TJ. I didn't have a home, my little ratty head told me. All grown up and no place to go.

I took my dinner break with a slice of double cheese and a root beer. I thought about taking up smoking. If I smoked, that would have been the perfect time for a cigarette. But cheese tastes nasty with smoke. The boss yelled at me, and I went back to work.

A family sat down in my section just before eight o'clock. I almost told them the kitchen was closed. I should have, but I didn't, because I felt bad for the kid. One look and you knew that he got the crap beat out of him a couple times a year, plus he got teased on the bus and in gym. It wasn't just the retainer, or the thick glasses, or the clueless clothes. It was the "please don't hurt me" look in his eyes. His dad was a taller, skinnier version of the son. I bet he went through the same torture when he was young, but he never figured out why the other kids picked on him.

When I see parents like that, I just want to smack them upside the head. How hard is it to buy your kid a shirt that doesn't scream, "I am a huge dorko! Please spit in my hair!"?

So I brought them menus and explained that no, we didn't have low-fat pizza. They ordered. I served. They ate. I cleared. They paid and left. I cleaned and cheered (to myself) because they were my last table of the night.

They came back fifteen minutes after we locked the front door. My first thought was food poisoning, but my second thought was no, food poisoning cases always took a couple hours to kick in.

My manager went to the door and talked to the dad. Then he filled me in on the problem.

Dorko Boy had lost his retainer.

Do you have any idea what that means?

I had to find his retainer.

In the Dumpster.

99.

The bus driver wouldn't let me on the bus because I reeked so bad. It was a long walk home. What if I had to walk back to our apartment from the restaurant at night? That would take hours, and I'd have to make it past the guys doing business at the corner of Hamilton and Pearce. Maybe I should ask if Ma could get me a job with the Transit Authority. Or if Dad could get me in as a dispatcher. Either way, I'd get free rides. It would be really cool if I could work downtown in City Hall or in one of the skyscrapers. I'd wear suits to work, and with my legs I could get away with miniskirts and heels, so every time I walked into a meeting all the executives would be like, "Whoa, who's the new girl?" and I'd be so prepared for the meeting it would blow them all away, and I'd get full benefits and a paid vacation and a company car, and I'd never have to walk home alone in the dark.

100.

I didn't pay attention to the announcements in Homeroom on Monday because I had to analyse another poem for English. This one was about the moon – dumb, but very short. Poems are short because nobody can keep up that level of stupidness for more than one page.

Nat wobbled into homeroom during announcements. She was determined to learn how to walk in those red high-heeled sandals. When the announcements were over, she burst into tears.

"Natalia," said Ms Jones-Atkinson. "What's the matter?"

"Blisters?" I asked. "Those shoes look small."

Nat shook her head, pointed at the speaker and sniffed.

I reached across and felt her forehead. No fever.

"It was something Mr Banks said," Lauren explained.

"T-t-tickets," Nat said.

Lauren gave her a tissue and she blew her nose.

"Prom tickets?" asked Ms J-A.

Nat nodded.

"Prom tickets are still available," I said, trying to be helpful and all.

Nat put her head on her desk.

"What did I say?" I asked.

Nat handed me that scary pink prom notebook, open to the ticket sales page. Lauren and I looked at it together. We had sold a total of 31 tickets. If we didn't make the minimum number, Banks was going to cancel, no discussion.

The minimum number was 100.

"Oh," I said.

"You have to do something," Lauren told me.

"That's enough about the prom," said Ms J-A. "It's time to get to heroin."

101.

I didn't do so good in my English presentation. Turned out the poet was not talking about the moon. She was talking about people or death. Or something.

Nat was so bummed about the whole ticket thing that I offered to meet with the custodians during Study Hall. I wound up buying them all Snickers bars, and they fished out the extension cords we needed, and the boss guy showed me the special covering they had for the gym floor so the high heels of us ladies wouldn't ruin it.

Ashley Hannigan, prom organizing queen. That was me. Turned out I was a natural at bossing people around.

I took the shortcut behind the gym to avoid Gilroy's office. It was always fun to watch somebody else being tortured by Mr Boyd, so I peeked in the doors. The students were supposed to be running laps, but instead they were shuffling around in groups, like a chain gang getting exercise in a jail.

Boyd jogged out of his office and blew his whistle. "All right, people, let's go! Two laps to warm up!"

This was the gym class with the so-called popular kids in it. I never understood that – how some kids got to be popular, and others didn't. I think it was something they decided that week in seventh grade when I was sick with pneumonia. Persia Faulkner, who was as close to Carceras royalty as you could get, was at the front of the pack. Persia and her girls looked at Boyd like he was a homeless guy bumming for quarters.

Boyd blew his whistle so hard I thought his brains were going to shoot out his ears. "Running!" he yelled. "I said running! Miss Faulkner, can we have some leadership here? Set an example, please. Pick up the pace."

Everyone looked to see what Persia did. She sighed like a diva forced to drink tap water, rolled her eyes, and moved her arms back and forth a little faster so it would look like she was making an effort to run.

"Thank you!" Boyd yelled.

I was stunned. *No, thank you, Mr Boyd!* I swear I heard angels sing and trumpets play, though that could have been the concert band practising down the hall. Of all the people in this sorry-ass school, it was a gym teacher who showed me what I had to do. And all those years I had been thinking that gym teachers were a total waste. *Wow.* Just goes to show you, doesn't it?

103.

I followed Persia into the bathroom after gym and waited for her outside her stall. She made a nasty stink doing her business in there, but I was smart enough not to say anything about it. I stood behind her while she washed her hands.

"You want something?" she finally asked.

"I need your help," I said.

"You got that right. Hand me a towel."

I explained what I wanted while Persia dried her hands.

"So?" she said.

"So don't you want to help out your classmates?"

"I excel at not giving a shit about y'all." She gave me the wet paper towel. "What's in it for me?"

"A good time. A senior prom. Night to remember, time of your life?"

She fished her lip liner out of her purse and leaned towards the mirror. "You'll have to do better than that."

"What do you want?"

She talked to the mirror while she outlined her lips. "Malcolm cancelled our limo when we heard the prom was off. He tried to get it back when we heard the prom was back on, but it was already taken by someone else. Nobody in the tri-state area has a limo available for Friday night. I refuse to show up to my senior prom in the back of Malcolm's mother's SUV."

"You're blowing off your prom because you don't have a classy ride? What about your dress? It'll go to waste."

She capped the lip liner. "Nothing I own goes to waste. We'll go clubbing instead."

"Does it have to be a limousine?"

"Are you deaf? What did I just tell you?"

"I mean, everybody gets a limo. Hell, even me and TJ are gonna have a limo."

156

"You still going with him?" She shook her head. "Girl, you a freak."

"What if I could get you a classic car, a ride that nobody else has?"

"Is it clean?"

"Sick clean. Ask Malcolm. You two will look like you're pulling up to the VMAs."

She smiled at herself to check her perfect teeth. "For real you can do this?"

"I swear. If I don't come through, you'll have me killed, so I ain't lying. You can make this happen, Persia. It's up to you."

She turned to look at me. "A'ight."

"Really? You'll help us?"

"You get me a cool car and the prom will rock. Now get lost before somebody sees me talking to you."

104.

Nat was still in a funk when we got to math. On top of all the prom stuff, I knew she was stressing about her grandmother. I wanted to tell her about my deal with Persia, but I didn't because she'd go off the deep end if my plan tanked.

The math sub had heard about the prom trouble. He decided to help us with our budget. Nat gave him the numbers we were working with, and he wrote them out on the board. Instead of asking for passes, most of our classmates hung around to see what all of this was costing us. The sub passed out calculators and everybody talked about what they were paying for, like Dalinda's three-hundred-dollar dress and Hector's seventy-dollar hat.

When Mr Gilroy walked in the door, he was shocked. I don't know what he had heard about this sub, but for sure he was not expecting to see all of us sitting in our chairs with calculators and paper and pencils, and the board covered with numbers.

"What are we working on?" Gilroy asked.

"Per centages and probability," said the sub.

After Gilroy left, Dalinda asked the sub what "probability" was.

"It's looking at your odds," he said. "Figuring out the chances of success."

"Success at what?" I asked.

"Pulling this thing off," he said. "The prom."

"So what are our chances?" Nat asked.

"We don't have enough data to calculate probability."

"That means you got *nada*," said Hector.

When the bell rang, I asked the sub if he could sign me in for detention without me showing up that day, because of the prom stuff. He said no problem. Then he asked me if the school's liability insurance would cover the prom.

"I don't know," I said.

"You can never have too much insurance. Stuff happens."

"Tell me about it. Stuff is going to happen to me if I don't get out of here."

"Have fun."

Nat made me go with her and Lauren and Aisha to a meeting with Principal Banks after school. The good news was that Banks had found a little extra money in his budget. He wanted it to go for prom favours, which are basically birthday party goodie bags for teenagers.

Just as he was about to tell us what he wanted us to buy, my new cell phone rang. I didn't know it was my phone because nobody had called me yet. I didn't even know my number.

Mr Banks lectured me about cell phone rules and inappropriate distractions while I tried to figure out how to turn the damn thing off, which I could not do, so Aisha took it out of my hand and pushed a button I didn't even see it was so small.

Nat and Banks agreed that the goodie bags could have bottles of bubbles and rave sticks and a picture frame. But the committee wanted each bag to have a garter with our school colours, and an etched shot glass, because that was "tradition".

And, Lauren added, we wanted condoms.

Mr Banks was cool about the shot glasses, not sure about the garters, and what you call closed-minded about condoms.

"No," he said. "Absolutely, positively not. We will not and cannot and shall not allow this to happen. Never. No."

"Mr Banks, that's a very negative attitude," I said. "We're talking about prom favours, right? If we pass out condoms, that would be a monster favour. We could get them in the school colours, that would be cool."

Nat kicked me.

Lauren quoted statistics about teen pregnancy rates and asked if the school district tracked the number of babies born nine months after prom season.

That's when my phone went off for the second time and Banks kicked me out.

It was cool to talk to TJ while I walked to my locker and got my stuff and went outside and sat on the steps. He had picked up some hours from Marty changing oil filters and his second Wal-Mart interview was the next morning. He did most of the talking, but I didn't mind, because his voice was so happy, and he sounded tall and awesome, and he was working so hard for us. When he asked me what was up, I told him about the meeting he got me kicked out of, and how Nat was wearing her prom shoes that were really stilts, and she needed ski poles or a walker to walk with so she didn't break her neck. He thought that was funny. He said he loved me and missed me.

106.

After school, I made Nat change into sneakers. We chased all over the city looking for deals on prom favours. You should have heard her flipping out on Banks about the garters and condoms.

No, you should not have heard it. You would have been as bored as I was.

I finally got sick of listening to her whine and dragged her into the free health clinic on Rush Street. The receptionist said she could only give us a dozen condoms, which sucked, but then one of the doctors heard us talking and he asked for our address. He graduated from Carceras, which blew me away, because I never figured somebody from our school could become a real doctor. I gave him my address at the apartment and he said he would see what he could do.

When we left, Nat said he was hitting on me. I punched her and said that was sick, because he had to be, like, thirty years old. *Ew*.

When I finally got home, there was laundry piled everywhere in the kitchen. My so-called prom dress, the one Ma scammed at the mall, was hanging off the kitchen door. She must have been showing it off again. Billy was drawing in his Spider-Man colouring book at the kitchen table. Nat's grandmother was sitting next to him sewing something.

"Where is everybody?" I asked.

"I dunno." Billy gave Spider-Man orange eyes.

"Who's watching you?"

He pointed his crayon at Grandma. "She is."

Grandma smiled at me. She hadn't put her teeth in. She patted Billy's head and gave him a kiss.

"Can you make her stop kissing me?"

"Probably not," I said.

Ma came in holding her purse and the car keys. "There you are. I thought you were never coming home."

"Do you think Grandma here has enough marbles to babysit?" I asked. "What if he decided to run with scissors or something?"

"She's not babysitting Billy. I'm babysitting her. The people who were watching her took her home before lunch. She kept getting in the bathtub with her clothes on. She came here and I gave her some ravioli. Since then she's just been sewing. It's a shame they have to put her in a home. She's not that bad when you get used to her."

I opened a package of Pop-Tarts. "They found a home already?" I whispered.

"You can speak up. She doesn't speak English, you know."

Grandma babbled again and took Billy's black crayon.

"That's sad," I said. "About the home, I mean."

Ma took a Pop-Tart from the box. "I know. I'm starting to like the old lady. Must be my hormones or something."

"Something."

Grandma picked up a purple crayon and coloured Spider-Man's shoes. Billy giggled.

Ma bit her Pop-Tart. "If Nat's back, why don't you take her home. Then you can carry the laundry to the car for me."

108.

I had a choice – go to the Laundromat with Ma, or stay home and put the boys to bed. I stayed home. Then Dad gave me the choice of taping drywall in the basement or putting the boys to bed. Great choices, huh?

I played three hands of poker with Steven and Shawn. The first two hands we played for M&Ms and I let them each win once, leaving me with only one piece of candy, a brown one. Then I upped the stakes – if they won, they'd each get twenty bucks. If I won, they had to go to bed in three minutes, lights out in ten.

They fell for it.

Two jacks and a pair of sevens later, I was sending them up to brush their teeth.

Billy was harder because he would only play Go Fish and that takes for ever. There was no way out of it.

"Okay, I'll read a story. What do you want?"

"Harry Potter."

"Nice try. Something shorter."

"Spider-Man and the Monsters."

"It'll give you nightmares."

"I like nightmares."

"Last chance, kid, or I'm turning out the light."

"Make up a story."

"What?"

"Make up a story. Like Dad does."

"I'm not good at making stuff up."

"You promised."

"What is it with everybody around here? Geez."

We shoved the dog off his bed, and Billy snuggled in next to me. He tucked Binky Rabbit under his arm and stuck his thumb in his mouth.

"I do not see that thumb in your mouth, do I?"

He shook his head.

"Okay, just so we're clear. Ma asks, I didn't see a thing. Move over a little, I can't breathe. All right. Once upon a time..."

The story started out like Beauty and the Beast, but I

gave Beauty a personal assistant and a chauffeur. Beauty ran into Cinderella at the mall and told her that with her eyes, she'd look great in a sky-blue dress with silver jewellery. They went to a spa and got facials and massages, and Cinderella got the prince to invite Beauty and the Beast with them on a double date out to dinner at a French restaurant with a champagne fountain and lobster. The more I talked, the easier it got, until they ended the night in a hot air balloon that landed on Rodeo Drive.

"And they shopped happily ever after," I said. "There. That didn't totally suck, did it?"

Billy was sound asleep. I didn't know if that meant that the story was so boring it knocked him out, or that it was so good it knocked him out. It didn't really matter. The boys were all down for the night, and me and Mutt had the TV to ourselves.

109.

School in May tended to be optional, especially if the sun was shining. That's why I was confused on Tuesday. The halls were crowded like it was September. And people were talking.

"Gonna have Masta Big…"

"…cooked up by a promoter…"

"…and then we get all this free food."

"…said she lined up a classic car."

"…and then we're going on a cruise."

"…roulette wheel, craps table…"

"…no, a boat cruise, on the river."

"I heard it'll be on all the cable channels."

"…something big…"

"…all a hoax, don't believe it…"

110.

Lauren and Nat took over health by telling Ms J-A about how Mr Banks wouldn't let us put condoms in the goodie bags for the prom. This made Ms J-A turn seven different shades of mad, and we were in for another condom lecture, though I shouldn't complain, because some kids in that class still didn't get it. I loved it when we got to talk about sex in class and not get in trouble for it, even if all we could talk about was the negatives: you know, don't get pregnant or your life is over, don't get HIV or your life is over, don't get an STD or your life is over and your crotch will stink and itch.

After the lecture, Ms J-A forced me go to the Media

Centre to deal with the mystery overdue book fines. They had sent me four notices, and now they were threatening to send dogs after me.

They used to call it the library, but after they stuck in a bunch of computers and ripped out the card catalogue, it was suddenly a Media Centre. The librarians were magically – *poof!* – turned into Media Centerians.

It was still a boring, boring, boring, boring room, no matter what they called it.

The Media Centerian guy wouldn't let me finish one single sentence. I gave him my student number and he printed out my account. He claimed I had borrowed five books *(five!!)* before Christmas, and I had to return them or pay for them.

I had never heard of the books or the authors. In fact, I was pretty sure I had never, ever borrowed anything, in my almost four years at Carceras. He checked his computer and said yes, the missing five were the first books I had ever borrowed. I tried whining and looking cute, but he acted like he didn't care.

"Books are expensive," he said.

"No shit," I said.

"We don't allow that language in here," he said.

"What about that freedom of speech thing?" I asked.

"It doesn't apply in high school. You don't have a choice, Miss Hannigan. You have to pay."

112.

The lunch line was buzzing. The kids waiting for pizza gossiped about who was asking who to the prom or waiting to be asked to the prom. The guys waiting for cheeseburgers were talking about the best place to go to dinner – restaurants that were cheap, classy, and would serve underaged teens, or not bitch if you brought your own bottle of Jack. Three girls at the salad bar were giggling about some dude in front of the candy machine, trying to get the nerve to ask him.

I bought a plate of french fries and a cup of ketchup.

Lauren and Monica were sitting behind the cash box. Next to them was a handmade sign:

PROM TICKETS GOING FAST!
GET YOURS B4 IT'S 2 LATE!!!

"What's going on?" I asked.

"I don't know what happened," Monica said. "Yesterday we couldn't give these things away. Today we can't sell them fast enough."

I sat next to Lauren and pushed my plate of fries where we could all reach them. "Did we make our quota?"

Lauren pointed at the list of ticket buyers with a fry. "We made it and then some. Right now we've got a third of the senior class coming, and a whole bunch more reserved tickets that they promised to buy by the end of school tomorrow."

Monica dipped her pinkie finger in the ketchup and sucked it off. "Ketchup is a vegetable, you know. Hardly any calories. Guess who was first in line today?"

I was pretty sure I knew, but I shrugged my shoulders.

"Persia Faulkner! Can you believe it? I can't believe it. Persia Faulkner."

"That's why we've had this run," Lauren said. "Where Persia leads, the masses follow. And by the way, Mon, ketchup has corn syrup in it. That means massive calories."

Monica pushed the ketchup away from her and pouted.

"What did Nat say?" I asked.

Lauren dropped out of the conversation to sell a pair of tickets to a couple of goths. Monica tilted her head to one side.

"I haven't seen Nat all day. Didn't you drive in with her?"

"Yeah, she was in health. She hasn't stopped by here?"

The goths slid away from the table. Lauren put their money in the box, grinning. "If all those freaks come, that's another dozen tickets. They move in a pack, you know."

"You seen Nat?" I asked.

"She had a meeting with the English teachers about PDAs. Last I saw she was hanging on the lockers trying to get down the hall in those damn shoes."

I dunked a couple fries in ketchup and ate them. "Maybe she went home to check on her grandma. My mom had to work, and there was nobody who could babysit her."

"Maybe she'll bring Granny's walker to help her with those shoes," Lauren said.

"Maybe I'll just stop eating totally," Monica said with a sigh.

113.

I got called into Mr Banks's office after lunch. At first, I thought I was getting nailed for my attitude in the Media Centre, but then I realized it could be worse. Did he know about my detention scam? That was more of a Gilroy thing, not a Banks thing. Was he still mad about the condoms?

The secretary pointed me to Banks's office. When I stepped through the door, Banks was typing on a keyboard and staring at his computer screen.

"Ashley. Have a seat, please. "

I sat.

He pushed his keyboard away. "We have a couple of crucial decisions that must be made immediately."

"Huh?"

"The commemorative glasses, for one. My secretary called around. Given your budget restrictions, we can't go as big as a milk or juice glass. I am concerned about the message sent by the smaller glasses, but if we call them commemoratives, we shouldn't hear too many complaints from the community."

He flipped a piece of paper on his desk. "And I still haven't received your complete security plan. We need to coordinate a meeting with Mr Gilroy, our head of security, and the township police department. Who knows, we might also consider notifying the sheriff's office, just in case. You can never be too secure, can you?"

I put my hand up. "Um, Mr Banks?"

"Yes?"

"With all respect, what the heck are you talking about?"

He scribbled a note on the paper and looked up. "Why, the prom, of course."

"Oh." I scratched an itch on my nose. "So why are you talking to me about it?"

"Because no one can seem to locate our Miss Shulmensky."

"Oh."

"Now Mr Gilroy says he has time available tomorrow at lunch if we can get the police chief in. If not, it'll have to be a phone conference."

I raised my hand again. It felt dumb, but I didn't know what else to do.

"Um, Mr Banks?"

"What is it now?"

"Why aren't you talking to Monica or Lauren? They've been on the prom committee all year. I'm just kind of like Nat's assistant, you know, got her back and everything. But I can't make decisions. I don't know nothing."

"Anything. You don't know anything. But I beg to differ. Natalia told me personally that you were number two in this operation and that if she were tied up, I could consult with you."

"Okay, that's nuts. How about we find Nat. She's way better at all this stuff."

He sighed. "She seems to be, ahh, we can't find her."

"Did you call her house?"

"Several times. And her father's emergency contact number. Do you know where she is?"

"I think so." I explained about her grandmother, how her brain was crumbling and all. "Maybe something happened. Maybe she..."

"Aaah. Possibly. I had no idea." He wrote another note on his pad. "Thank you for telling me."

I pushed the chair back.

"Hold on," he said. "What about the glasses? And security?"

"Order the glasses. Call them what you want. And

make Mr Gilroy call the police chief himself. You're the boss, aren't you? He pushes you around too much. Can I go now?"

He blinked slowly. "One more thing. A personal comment, if I may. I was worried we were going to lose you this year. You'd be amazed at how many kids drop out in the months and weeks before they graduate."

"Tell me about it."

"Yes, well, you're still on thin ice, what with your grades and spotty attendance. We have to adhere to our standards, you know, regardless of enthusiastic extracurricular effort."

"The tassel is worth the hassle, Mr Banks."

"Truer words were never spoken. Thank you for your assistance in these matters. And please keep me informed about Miss Shulmensky's family situation."

I stood up, nodded like I was listening, and reached for the door.

"Oh, and Ashley—"

Now what? I stopped by the door.

"What do you think of the new math substitute?"

"The insurance guy? He's a hardass. Shouldn't be allowed near kids."

Mr Banks smiled. "Glad to hear it. When you see Natalia, remind her that we'll need an authorized excuse form tomorrow."

Cell phones are no good if the person you're calling doesn't answer. I dialled Nat's number so many times the battery wore down. At least I think it was the battery. TJ said the phone didn't come with an instruction book.

As soon as the last bell of the day rang, I bolted. Didn't stop running until I got to Nat's.

I got there just in time to help her father carry her inside.

"It was the shoes," Nat said slowly. She was lying on her couch with her right leg propped up on pillows. A light blue cast started at her ankle and kept going until it disappeared under her shorts.

"I came home to check on Grandma, then boom, the shoes and the stairs." She waved her hand at the staircase. "Shooze 'n' stairs. Stairsnshooze..."

"How many painkillers did they give you?" I asked.

She shrugged and giggled. "Don't know." She pointed to her cast. "Look, it matches my dress. You should break your leg, too, Ash. Then we could be twins."

Nat's father came downstairs with an afghan. He covered Nat with it. "Poor baby."

Nat closed her eyes.

"How long until she can gimp around?" I asked.

"No walking. She needs a wheelchair."

"Great!" I said. "So she'll be at school tomorrow. That's awesome. I can drive her if you want, if she'll let me use her car. And I'm sure they'll let me push her around from class to class. They'll give us the elevator key so we can get up to the third floor."

Nat's dad sat down in the chair across from me. "Ashley." His voice was slow and quiet, like he was getting ready to talk to someone who wasn't quite there or didn't speak English. "Natalia will not be at school tomorrow. Maybe Thursday, for a little while. But I'm not promising you."

"But she has to be. The prom. What are we going to do?"

"Dance, dance, dance," sang Nat, who had pulled the afghan up over her face.

"Everybody's counting on her."

"The prom will be fine. You and the other girls will do a good job. It's just a dance."

Nat's hand came out from under the afghan. It pointed to the pile of books at the bottom of the stairs. "Take the notebook. The pink one."

Mr Shulmensky went through the pile. "This one?" he asked.

No answer from the afghan. She was out cold.

"That's it," I said as he handed it to me. The thing weighed a ton. "Who's going to take care of her tomorrow? I could come and stay with her."

"No, it's fine. I'll take a sick day."

"What about Grandma?"

He pointed overhead. There was a deep hum from the second floor, a vibrating machine sound like a metal cat purring. "My mother's sewing. Natalia will sleep all afternoon. You might as well go home."

As he closed the door, Nat started singing again.

116.

The pink notebook was the biggest pain I ever had in my life. As soon as I touched it, the curse entered my veins. I was doomed.

Nat's to-do list went on for pages, including:

1. Custodians – electric load?
4. Pack goodie bags
9. Confirm required playlist w/ DJ – represent all ethnic groups and music tastes!
13. More pastry for custodians
14. Extra take-home pastry for chaperones
15. Paper flowers for chaperones?
24. Who will direct traffic – limo drop-off?
29. Fire marshal meeting
30. Clean-up crew needs bribe
34. Do we need coat check???

42. Is there money for helium to blow up balloons?

46. Thong discussion

I should have strapped on Nat's shoes and thrown myself down a flight of stairs.

Instead, I turned to a blank page and wrote out my own list:

1. Call work – stomach flu
2. Ma – no babysitting!!!!!!!!
3. Dad – need to get car for Persia $$$???
4. TJ – MUST have tux!! MUST pay for dinner! (not hoagies) New apt. when??

117.

It was two-thirty Tuesday afternoon. Prom started at seven-thirty Friday night. We had almost eighty hours to pull this thing off, as long as we didn't sleep.

I called Lauren and had her grab everyone for an emergency prom meeting. Six girls showed. I gave each one of them their own list of things to do from the pink notebook. I wound up being stuck with the gross stuff, like dealing with teachers and Gilroy and administrators. I told the girls that if I had to deal with that dumbass, I would quit right there, right then. Lauren volunteered for Gilroy duty. He liked her. She was a success story.

By the end of the meeting, we had seventy-five hours left.

118.

Wednesday was a blur of phone calls and begging and making notes and making promises and getting promises. Every time I crossed an item off the list in the notebook, I had to write down something new. We bagged the idea of a coat check. The fire marshal was cool with our plan. Helium balloons were out. Streamers were in – the cheerleaders had extras from a pep rally that got cancelled. On and on and on. I didn't have time for lunch and forgot to eat dinner – actually forgot. It suddenly made sense how all those girls in the prom magazines got skinny enough to fit into their dresses.

Ma kept my dress hanging in the kitchen where she could talk to it and touch it as often as she wanted. Whatever kept her happy and off my case. Dad scored the car he promised for Persia Faulkner. I gave Malcolm the details, he met the guy, saw the car, and told me that if I ever needed anything in the way of air-conditioning duct cleaning, he could get me a good deal with his dad. I was just happy Persia wasn't going to poke out my eyeballs with her nail file.

I was on the phone to Nat every hour. The best time to talk to her was twenty minutes after she took her pain meds, after the pain stopped, but before the serious buzz began. I really should have only called her every four hours, but it was fun to listen to her when she was all messed up. She kept her grandmother baking pastries and was able to make a couple of calls for me. She also explained the whole "thong discussion". I told her that it was nobody's business what underwear girls had on, and it didn't matter if they banned thongs in the Midwest somewhere, this is Pennsylvania, yo, cradle of liberty and all that, and we were not checking thongs at the prom.

Ashley Hannigan, prom organizing queen and defender of thongs. Who knew?

The worst thing was when Nat's so-called prom date Jason gave me a note in the hall that said he couldn't take Nat to the prom, because wheelchairs freaked him out, because his brother was in a wheelchair before he died of blood cancer. I heard from Monica that he was taking Evelyn Choo, who had two working legs and one of the cutest butts in school.

I waited until Nat was totally cooked on her meds to drop the bomb. She laughed and said she was pretty certain Jason was gay, and the only reason she was going with him was because she knew he wouldn't bug her to get laid. Then she cried because she was going to be stuck in a wheelchair for her night of magic moments.

You can learn a lot about your best friend with the aid of legal pharmaceuticals.

119.

TJ showed up all excited after dinner. He pulled me out on the front porch to talk.

First, we had a long kiss. Then he said, "You are the most babelicious, awesome girlfriend in the history of the world. Of the universe."

"Wow," I said. "What finally convinced you?"

"This." He picked up a cardboard box from the porch swing. "It came to the apartment."

"You opened it?"

"Yeah."

"But it has my name on it."

"So? It's *our* place, right?" He reached in and pulled out a handful of condoms in colourful wrappers. He poured them back into the box like they were gold coins and kissed me again.

"Um, TJ, you don't understand."

"Ashley Hannigan, you are the hottest."

The look on his face reminded me of a Labrador retriever again.

"Give me that." I snatched the box out of his hands. There was a short note inside from the doctor at the free clinic. He wrote that I couldn't tell anyone where these condoms came from or he'd get in trouble. There were one thousand condoms in the box. The doc hoped that would be enough.

I looked at TJ. "These aren't for us, moron, they're for the prom."

He looked like I had smacked him on the nose with a rolled-up newspaper. "Can't we keep some of them?"

"How many do you want to keep?"

"How about, ah, two hundred."

"Ten."

He sighed, grabbed a huge handful from the box, and stuffed them in his pocket.

I folded up the flaps of the box. TJ wrapped his arms around my waist and pulled me close. "Want to come back with me and use a couple?"

"I can't. I only have forty-seven hours left. You can stay if you want, but if you do, you have to help us fold the origami flowers."

Just before I got to school the next morning, a 32 bus pulled into the kerb right next to me. The door popped open, but nobody got off.

"Ashley? Is that what you're wearing today? You're going to catch your death."

That voice again.

You think it's embarrassing when your mother pulls the minivan over to talk to you, try having her behind the wheel of a full-sized city bus. There was no point running into the school and hiding. She'd find me.

I turned to see her in the driver's seat, her belly bumping up against the wheel. "Yes, this is what I'm wearing, Ma. It's summer."

"It's only May and it's chilly. Come here, young lady."

I stepped up into the stairwell. The passengers stared. A couple waved at me.

"You remember Mrs Meadows?" Ma asked.

"Hello, Ashley," said the black lady sitting behind the driver's seat.

"Hello, Mrs Meadows," I said. She was a regular. "Nice to see you again."

"I hear exciting things about your prom," Mrs Meadows said.

"I'm sure," I said.

Ma pulled the sweater off the back of her seat. "Put

this on so you don't look cheap. Your boobs are spilling out."

Mrs Meadows smiled. "Your mother has a point, dear."

I folded the sweater on top of my books.

"Don't forget you need to make time for pictures tomorrow night," Ma said. "Your aunts are all coming with their cameras."

"Maaa!"

"Pictures are important," Mrs Meadows said.

"And your aunt Sharon wanted me to ask if you filled out those applications she got for you."

"I've been a little busy, don't you think?"

"I hear they're hiring again at the soup factory," Mrs Meadows said.

The school bell rang.

"I'm going to be late," I said.

"Did TJ pick up his tux yet?" Ma asked.

"I don't know."

"Well, you better check," Ma said. "Knowing him, he'll 'forget' to pick it up or some other crap."

Mrs Meadows shook her head slowly. "I've heard about that boy."

"She talks to you about TJ?"

"Mrs Meadows understands," Ma said.

"I raised seven of my own," Mrs Meadows said.

"Hey, lady," shouted a guy from the back. "I got places to go."

Mrs Meadows reached forward and patted my arm. "Have fun at your dance, dear."

Ma pushed in the clutch. "You better hurry or you'll be late."

"Right."

"And put on that sweater."

"Whatever, Ma."

The rest of Thursday was just like Wednesday, only busier. But at least I was beginning to win the Battle of the Pink Notebook. Now when I crossed off one of the to-do things, another one didn't pop up.

People in the halls were saying "yo" and "hey" to me. A couple white girls had sunburns from tanning salons. The cafeteria sold out of lettuce and bottled water to all the ladies trying to drop twenty pounds in two days. Monica said we sold more than 150 tickets – enough to pay the DJ and buy soda and real food, instead of making us beg our moms to cook.

Having to miss so many classes to get all the prom stuff done was a definite plus in my book, but things were so under control, I actually made it to gym on Thursday.

Go me.

Gym was cool because Boyd couldn't make us do

anything. The custodians were laying down the floor covering, helped by a bunch of the guys from the class. I convinced Boyd to let the rest of us hang the streamers. I wanted the lights to go up, too, but I was afraid if we hung them too soon, they'd get stolen. Miss Felony Crane showed us you can't be too careful with teachers, especially the ones still in grad school.

I had my hands full of purple streamers and tape when Boyd yelled at me that I had been called down to the principal's office.

122.

When I walked into Banks's office, the first thing, the only thing I saw, was my best friend, out of the house for the first time since her accident.

"Nat!"

She was sitting her wheelchair, the cast sticking straight out, covered with the old afghan from her house. Her eyes were uncrossed and she looked sad, but you had to figure that made sense.

"Whassup? You here for the rest of the day? Can I push her around?" I asked.

"Have a seat," Banks said from his chair. His computer was turned off this time.

"You hurting?" I asked Nat. "Should you be here? I

was coming over after school to fill you in. We are rocking the house. Almost everything is done. That reminds me, Mr B. The DJ signed your 'no drugs, no booze' agreement. Lauren will drop it off later."

"Please," Banks said. "Sit down, Ashley."

That's when my Spidey-sense tingled. Something was wrong in Promland. "Is this about the condoms again? I was going to talk to you about that."

"Please read this." Banks handed me a piece of paper.

It was a list of students who were banned from Senior Activities because they cut class, blew off detention, didn't pay fines, and whatnot. The list of names filled the page.

An air conditioner kicked in and a breeze blew across the room.

I looked at Nat. "Was this in the notebook? Did we forget to take care of something?"

"That's not it," she said.

The only sounds were the phone ringing out on the secretary's desk and the clock ticking on the wall behind me. I shivered.

"You're on the list, Ash," Nat said. "They won't let you go."

"What?"

Banks straightened the pens on his desk. "I'm afraid your own actions have banned you from the prom, Ashley."

The words didn't make sense. Nothing was making

sense. I couldn't find my name on the list until Nat rolled over and pointed it out to me. I was squeezed in between Makesh Hall and Ian Hansen. Still, it didn't sink in.

"I'm not going?"

"We can't make an exception," Banks said.

"I tried to tell him," Nat said. "We wouldn't be having this prom if it weren't for you."

"But I cut class to make the prom happen. I had to."

"Even if we eliminated the cuts this week, you have dozens of detentions to make up. Mr Gilroy assured me that the two of you had several discussions about this. You have to take responsibility for your actions."

"Gilroy won't budge," Nat said. "He said you were too high-profile now to cut you a break."

I looked at the list again. I knew Ian. We had been in Biology together. He broke out in hives a lot. I shivered again and put on my mother's sweater, which I had been dragging around all day along with the pink notebook.

"District policy, you understand."

But it bugged me that I didn't know this guy, this Makesh Hall. Was he new? How could there be somebody who got in as much stupid trouble as I did, and I didn't know his name? How many other Makeshes were there?

"You have killer library fines, and you have a record number of detentions, Ash. What were you thinking?"

The sweater was a little prickly, but it smelled like Ma: laundry soap, bleach, and peach body lotion.

"If we make one exception, we have to make others. Rules are rules."

I was out the door before I realized I was moving.

Nat tried to follow me, but she couldn't turn her wheelchair fast enough. "Where are you going? Ash? Ashley?"

123.

Once upon a time there was a girl who screwed up everything.

124.

I walked out of the building. I walked to the bus stop on the corner. I got on the first bus that showed up. Didn't check to see where it was going. I just got on. Sat down. Rode to Olney Terminal, where I got off.

I crossed the lot to another bus. Handed the driver my transfer. Couldn't sit down because the bus was crowded with tired people. Every time a seat opened up, an old lady would get on, or some ancient guy with a cane and no teeth, and of course, they got the open seat.

We drove south, way south, past Temple, past the churches on Broad, past the clinics, the wig shops, check-cashing places, past BK and KFC and Mickey D's. More tired people got on the bus, got off the bus, walked on the sidewalks home to dinner and maybe a drink. We passed City Hall and hurried through the nice part of the city with glass-fronted hotels and restaurants with candles and the ugly new concert hall.

I buttoned the sweater and stared at the ads above the bell cord: domestic violence hotline, a play I never heard of, a poster in a language I couldn't read. Across from me, a white lady with over-permed hair and a nurse's uniform was reading a book to her daughter. Next to them, a college-looking Hispanic guy dozed, his head tilted backwards, earphones plugged in good and tight.

I must have fallen asleep, too. Next thing I knew, the driver hissed air out of his brakes and shouted "Airport! Last stop!"

I rubbed my eyes. No nurse. No college guy.

"Let's go, sweetheart!" The driver stared at me in his rearview mirror and pointed to the open door.

"I don't want to get off here."

"You don't got a choice. I'm back to the garage as soon as you walk down them steps."

"But this isn't my stop."

"And I'm supposed to care? Next bus back into town will be here in forty-five minutes."

"My mother's a bus driver!"

"And my mother's the Queen of England. Have a nice night."

I had never been on an aeroplane. Always wanted to. My family couldn't afford to leave the state. We sure as hell couldn't afford to leave the ground. And airports were for other people, rich people, people going places, you know?

I walked in.

It was not what I thought it'd be. It was just as crowded as school, except instead of backpacks, people dragged huge suitcases on wheels. The security guards were in shape and intense. I thought for sure the security cameras had zeroed in on me as the only person who didn't belong there, the only fake. But nobody tackled me.

I followed the crowd up an escalator to the long line in front of the metal detectors. Again – just like school. When I finally got to the front, a tired Asian lady in a dumpy blue polyester suit and crappy shoes asked for my ticket. I told her I just wanted to see the planes and no, I didn't have a ticket. She stared at me in exactly the same way as the sales ladies at Bloomingdale's who know that you don't have any money so you might as well leave before you accidentally shoplift a fifty-dollar bracelet.

She kicked me out of the line.

I bought a soda and a packet of cashews and stared at the departure and arrival monitors. I hadn't heard of half of those places: Burlington, Grand Rapids, Ottawa, White Plains. The people standing around me knew. They were so busy with their rolling suitcases and their IDs and their tickets to God-knows-where, they couldn't even see me.

No, wait. Cancel that. They could see me. They were staring at me.

"Is that your phone?" asked a lady with overplucked eyebrows.

"My phone? I don't have a phone," I said.

"You sure?"

"My phone. Wait. I do have a phone."

The lady backed away from me and I opened my purse. The phone was buried under gum wrappers and tissues. The screen flashed *TJ Barnes. TJ Barnes. TJ Barnes.*

I answered.

Guess who.

TJ was all meet-me-at-the-apartment – I-scored-some-dope.

I was all my-life-sucks-we-can't-go-to-prom.

He was all that-is-so-awesome-I-looked-like-a-dork-in-the-tux-I'll-come-get-you-let's-get-high.

I was all not-in-a-party-mood-can't-you-tell-I'm-pissed-why-are-you-buying-dope-we-need-furniture.

He got all why-you-bitchin'-me-out-are-you-on-the-rag.

I don't know what came over me. Maybe the airport

X-ray machines gave off brain tumor waves or something. I dropped the phone in a trash can and headed for the escalator that would take me back down to ground level.

The sun was setting by the time I finally got home. The boys were watching a war on TV with the sound turned off. Mutt was curled up in the corner, his nose under his tail.

"You're in trouble," Billy said.

"Where you been?" Shawn asked.

"Ma's crying," Steven said.

"Why?"

There was hammering in the basement and Dad's voice. "Goddamnit!"

"She's upset," Shawn said.

"About the prom," Steven added.

Two heavy feet hit the floor above us. "Is that Ashley?" Ma called.

Before I could bribe them to keep their mouths shut and run out to catch the next bus to anywhere, Billy yelled, "She's baaaa-aack!"

The hammering stopped.

"Get out while you can," Shawn whispered.

Dad came up from the basement and Ma came down

from her bedroom. They met in the dining room. Billy unmuted the TV and the sounds of the battle exploded in the room.

"Oh, baby!" Ma blubbered.

"Your mother's been worried sick," Dad said.

Ma rolled across the room like a Humvee and threw her arms around me, smearing her tears and her mascara all over my face. "I'm so sorry. I'm so, so, sorry."

I patted her back. "It's not that big a deal."

"What are you, nuts?" Dad asked.

"I was so worried you weren't coming home," Ma said. She wiped her nose on my T-shirt and laid her head on my shoulder. "I called everybody we know."

"Here." Dad handed Ma the Kleenex box. She took a handful and sank into the recliner. Steven dove out of the chair just in time.

"Ma, settle down, it's not that big a deal. I don't care about the prom. It doesn't matter."

She waved the Kleenex at me and sobbed. "You're lying to protect my feelings!"

"Stop making your mother cry. And turn that thing down, Shawnie."

Shawn didn't move.

"I'm trying to make her feel better," I said.

"Stop yelling, George."

"I ain't yelling!"

Ma blew her nose like an elephant. "You were going to

193

look so beautiful, Ash. For once in your life, you were going to be a real princess in pink. And I ruined it for you."

"You're going off the deep end here, Ma. You should lie down."

Dad grabbed the remote from Shawn and muted the war. "Mary Alice, look. We'll find another dress. I don't know why you women get so obsessed about dresses, for Christ's sake. It's not like you totaled the car, is it? I know some guys down at The Haystack, they'll lend me the money. Just stop crying, Mary, please. You're killing me with those tears."

Ma gulped and sniffed. Dad walked over to the recliner and brushed her hair off her face. She leaned her head against his hip. We had half a second of quiet.

"Hold on," I said. "What happened to my dress?"

Ma wailed, fought her way out of the recliner and waddled into the kitchen.

"Whadja do that for?" Dad asked.

"What?"

Ma came back to the living room, her tears falling on the prom dress in her hands. On what used to be my prom dress. She shoved it at me.

"I ruin everything," she cried.

"I got to hang drywall," Dad said. "Call me when it's over."

I shook out the dress. The pink was faded and blotchy and stained with thick purple and black streaks.

194

"I don't know what happened," Ma said. "It got into one of the baskets I took to the laundromat."

"Along with some crayons," said Shawn.

I rubbed my fingernail on a black streak. "Crayon?"

Ma sniffed. "There must have been bleach in the machine, too, I honestly don't know, maybe I'm losing my marbles."

Steven handed her a Kleenex and she blew her nose again. She gave the wet tissue back to him. He tossed it behind the couch.

I folded the dress up. "Chill, Ma. It doesn't matter."

"I ruin the most important night of your life and it doesn't matter? You're just trying to make me feel better."

I picked the crayon wax under my fingernail. "Um, Ma? I can't go to the prom."

"I know! I ruined it!"

Steven handed her the box of Kleenex and opened his book.

"No, listen. Stop wailing and listen to me. I can't go. The principal won't let me. I have too many detentions."

Ma sniffed. "Huh?"

I explained the whole mess and why I took off after school, and I gave her the name of the bus driver who was rude to me when he dumped me at the airport. By the time I was finished, she had stopped crying, which was a relief.

"So you see, the dress doesn't matter, 'cause I can't go. It's over. I'm beat, Ma. I'm going to bed."

I slept like a dead person. When I finally woke up, it was quarter after ten in the morning and Binky Rabbit was on the pillow next to me.

Being in the house alone felt like waking up in a Stephen King movie where you are the only person left on the planet and you don't know why. I turned the TV on to The Weather Channel and cranked the volume so the quiet house didn't freak me out. I ate a peanut butter and grape jelly sandwich.

I didn't notice Ma's note until I poured a giant glass of orange juice. *Ash – I called you in sick to school. Do me a favour and get those boxes out of the attic.*

To get to our attic, you had to drag the step stool to the second floor, stand on it and reach up on tiptoe to pull down the folding stairs from the ceiling. Once the stairs were down, I snuck up there, hunched over so I didn't whack my head. I felt like I was in a dollhouse, only all the dolls had been thrown away.

The attic smelled hot and old. I used to like to play there when I was a kid, but now it gave me the creeps.

The three boxes Ma wanted were hiding under a heap of green plastic Christmas decorations. I carried them one at a time down the folding stairs, then down the real stairs to the living room. Stacked against the wall behind the boxes were the pieces of the crib that we had all slept in when we were babies. It took five trips to get the whole thing down to the porch. Maybe Dad had some extra paint I could use to make it nicer. Just because a kid is the last one in a family doesn't mean it should have an ugly crib.

128.

I was able to ignore the phone the first fifty times it rang, but after that it got on my nerves so I answered it.

"Jesus, Ash, don't do that."

"Don't do what, Ma, pick up the phone?"

"Don't scare me like that."

"Ma, how can I be scaring you? You ain't even here."

"You didn't pick up the phone."

"Yeah, I did. That's what you're talking into right now. A phone."

"Don't get smart with me, young lady."

"Okay, Ma, I'll stay stupid. Was there a reason you called, or did you just feel like bitching?"

"I wanted to make sure you were okay."

"I'm not, but that's okay. I got the boxes down."

"Do me a favour and wash them."

"The boxes?"

"The clothes in the boxes. Duh, Ashley."

"Can't. The washer is broken."

"Your dad got it working after you went to bed last night."

"No more Laundromat?"

"Don't get me started. Joanie and Sharon think we should sue that place."

"Why?"

"For ruining your dress. Pain and suffering. Loss of a significant life event."

Ma watched too much Court TV.

129.

The laundry room was at the bottom of the basement steps. I dumped the baby clothes out on the floor, sorted the darks and the lights, and stuffed the first load into the machine. I set the temp dial to cold and the cycle dial to delicate and started the machine. I didn't think of the fabric softener until I closed the lid. Ma always used fabric softener on the baby clothes.

Dad had strung old sheets to separate the laundry room from the rest of the basement. I pushed the sheets aside without thinking.

There it was.

No, not the fabric softener.

My room. My new room. My soon-to-be-room because I, me, Ashley Hannigan, was going to live in my parents' basement, probably for ever. Dad had finished drywalling the front and back walls, and except for the big hole towards the bottom of the front wall, he did a good job. There were two barred windows set high in the side wall that faced Nat's house. The floor was concrete, one corner stained dark blue from a kicked-over paint can. The tools Dad borrowed were piled in the middle of the floor, along with some coiled-up wire and my old boom box.

The washing machine started beating itself up. The load was unbalanced, maybe, or it was breaking again. I let the sheets drop, walked back to the washing machine, and pulled out the cycle dial. I reached into the wet clothes and moved them around, then started it up again, pushing in the dial.

Nothing happened.

I pulled it out. Nothing.

Pushed it in.

Nothing.

I turned the dial an itty-bitty bit to the right and pushed. The washer buzzed like a security alarm. I couldn't make it stop. I pushed, pulled, twisted, punched buttons and finally, I kicked that stupid-ass machine, I kicked it as hard as I could. I held on to the sides so it couldn't run away and I kicked it again because it was broken and it wouldn't shut up and all I was trying to do was to help and I broke it and all the clothes would be ruined proving once again that I was stupid and I kicked it again and cursed it and kicked and kicked and motherfucking bastard not gonna let me go to the stupid effing dance after I worked so hard for everybody else to have a good time and look so good and be all elegant and princess and grown-up with a limo and flowers and a pink satin gown that swirled when I twirled and I kicked that fucking machine because I was going to be a rat in this basement or I was going to be a baby mama in a grease hole with a stupid boyfriend who thought popcorn was food and I kicked the machine so hard it almost tipped over and the electric plug pulled out of the wall and the buzzing stopped.

130.

I sat down in the dirty baby clothes and cried like I hadn't cried for a long time.

My foot really hurt.

131.

Don't know how long I was down there. Long enough for my big toe to swell up like an overcooked hot dog.

I didn't move until Ma came home, then I limped upstairs and helped her unpack the groceries.

When she saw me limping, she made me sit down, then she sat next to me and yanked my foot into her lap. Raise four kids and you know more than most E.R. docs. Ma ran her fingers along the top of my foot. "Can you wiggle your toes?"

I tried. "A little."

She moved them a lot more than a little.

"Ow! That hurts."

She sat back. "Do I want to know how this happened?"

"I kicked the washer."

"You ... kicked..."

"Don't laugh. It's not funny."

"Did it jump you? Pull a gun?"

"See, now you're making fun of me."

"And now you're smiling. Nothing's broken, Jackie Chan." She went to the freezer and took out a bag of frozen peas, which she tossed to me. "Stick that on your foot. Want some ice cream?"

"I think I killed the washer, Ma. For good. There's a load of baby clothes in there soaking wet."

She took the pistachio ice cream out of the freezer, two spoons out of the drawer, and sat next to me. "Something is always broken. Most things can be fixed." She handed me a spoon. "Eat some ice cream. That usually helps."

Mid-afternoon I went to Nat's to help her get ready. With me not going because Gilroy was a jerk, and Nat going to the prom with her father because Jason was a jerk, it was almost as depressing in her bedroom as it was in our kitchen. I did an awesome job on Nat's hair, but she didn't want any sparkles glued to her neck or cleavage, and she couldn't choose between Pink Prism or Mocha Mirage for her nails, so I ended up giving her French tips, which is the most boring thing possible you could do for a prom, if you ask me, but Nat wasn't asking.

We stared hard at the wheelchair and talked about dressing it up with ribbons or extra fabric her grandmother had, but in the end, she said forget about it. Her butt was already sore from sitting in the damn thing and she didn't think they'd be staying late.

She took a couple of phone calls from Lauren and Monica about last-minute details. That was when I was working on her toenails. They were Steel Magic, by the way. Looked good with the light blue cast, kind of contrasty and hip.

She hung up the phone. "The DJ's there."

"Good."

"The food is all laid out."

"Good."

"They're all bummed you can't go."

I blew on her toes.

"That tickles," she said.

"Good."

She threw cotton balls at my head. "Your mom is right. You and TJ should go out someplace nice tonight. It'd be better than staying at home feeling sorry for yourself."

"I don't feel sorry for myself. I'm over it. I didn't want to go in the first place, remember?"

"So why are you flipping out?"

"What are you talking about, flipping out? I'm not flipping out, I'm doing your damn toes, that's what I'm doing, that's not flipping out."

"Oh, please." She rolled her wheelchair backwards. "You've been pouting since you walked in. Ditch that trashy tube top, get out the red lipstick, and make TJ spend some money on you for a change. Make a night of it, Ash. If you don't do it tonight, when will you?"

"Shut up."

"What are you afraid of? Having fun?"

I put the Steel Magic polish on her desk. "No."

"Yes, you are. I double-dog dare you."

"Shut up, Shulmensky. It's time to go."

133.

Half the neighbourhood – my parents, Grandma Shulmensky, the Ciangalella family, the Brewsters from two doors down, Miss Patsy and her twins – they were all standing on the sidewalk when Mr S. carried Nat to their car. They oohed and aahed about her dress, her hair, and her toenails. She did look good, got to give her credit. Especially the toenails.

Mr S. went back inside for her purse (beaded) and shawl. I helped Nat get comfortable in the front seat.

"Did you take your pain pill?" I asked.

"Yep."

"Did you double up like I suggested?"

"No. I don't want to spend my prom in a coma, thank you."

"I still think it was a good idea." We watched her wiggle her toes. "Your dress looks great, even with you sitting down."

"Grandma knows from sewing. Tell your mom thanks again for watching her tonight." She looked at her fingernails. "Grandma likes you, you know."

"Does that mean I have to take her swimming?"

"Shut up. She told me that you're a great woman and you can do a lot more than you think you can. End of speech."

I watched the pigeons sitting on the electric wires crap on my dad's taxi. "Shut up, yourself. You lied. You took that extra pill."

She gave me a little shove. "Find your boyfriend and go dancing. Okay?"

"I don't dance."

"You're wrong about that, too. Seeya-bye."

I sat next to Ma on the porch swing.

"Ain't that sweet, Nat taking her dad," Ma said. "Is that a Russian thing?"

"Don't be silly," I said. "Jason backed out at the last minute. Nat didn't have much to choose from."

Mutt barked at a squirrel across the street. Ma patted his head and he settled down at her feet with a little groan.

"I forgot to give Nat the condoms," I said.

"When you were little you had that lemonade stand on the corner, remember? Maybe you should open a condom stand outside the high school."

"Not a bad idea."

Ma grunted and put her feet up on the dog. "If these ankles swell any more, I'll be able to walk on water. Look at them – freaking pontoons."

"I don't want to look at your feet."

"Then close your eyes."

The swing creaked as we rocked. "Where did Dad go?"

Ma smiled. "He had an errand. Knight in shining armour kind of thing."

"Spare me."

"If you're going to be cranky, make yourself useful. Fish the baby clothes out of the washer, wring them good, and hang them on the line."

"Yes, Your Highness."

I swear she chuckled when I went inside.

135.

The basement was cold and damp. I tried to open up the two little windows in my so-called future "bedroom" but the locks were rusted shut. I could have banged them open with a hammer and a screwdriver, but I didn't have the energy. I just wanted some fresh air.

All over town, girls were pinning on corsages and boys were hiding their hard-ons, and parents were smiling and worrying. I wondered if the DJ had turned up stoned, and if the streamers had stayed up, and if the bathrooms were going to flood, if we had bought enough soda, if there would be a fight, if Gilroy would bring in cops to close the place down early, if anybody would miss me. I'd have to wait until Monday and hear about it all over and over and over and over again.

Monday was going to suck, hands down. If I prayed hard enough, maybe I could get hit by a meteor or an out-of-control street sweeper. That way I wouldn't have to hear about how much fun it was, how awesome it was, how much I missed. On the other hand, if I got accidentally killed, I'd probably wind up in Purgatory, next to some old windbag who would spend the next thousand years complaining about her haemorrhoids.

A pair of feet skipped past the windows. Notice that I said skipped, not walked or ran or shuffled.

I moved two cans of paint under the window to stand on for a better look.

Those were Grandma Shulmensky's skipping feet. If my grandma Hannigan skipped like that, her arthritis or her lumbago or her disks would have acted up and she would have needed four or five gin and tonics. But the crazy bat next door was skipping.

I grabbed the bars and pulled myself up so I could see into the backyard. Grandma Shulmensky turned on their sprinkler. She clapped her hands when the water came spraying out, clapped and hopped and skipped, her face tilted back, catching the rays of the sun and the *whoosh*, *whoosh*, *whoosh* spray of the water.

136.

When I took the wet baby clothes outside, Grandma S. turned off the sprinkler and scurried into her own house, like I had spooked her or something. The clothesline was the scene of a massacre, a couple dozen action figures my bloodthirsty brothers left dangling. I piled the soldiers by the steps and started hanging up the faded onesies, new-baby sized.

Grandma S. came back outside with her robe on over her bathing suit. I watched her out of the corner of my eye as I pinned a tiny Eagles shirt to the line. She walked through our gate and set her laundry basket on the ground next to me.

"Am I hanging up your clothes, too?" I asked.

Grandma didn't have her teeth in. She chattered away like a monkey and did a few steps of her sprinkler dance.

"Ma!" I shouted. "Do we have any ravioli?"

Ma called through the screen door. "I ate the last can for breakfast. What's she doing?"

"Nothing. Don't worry."

"Hurry up. Your aunts are going to be here in a minute."

"Maaa! Why?"

"They're coming over to cheer me up, since you got kicked out of the prom."

"Oh, yeah, they'll be a real help." I wrung the water out of a thin baby blanket and draped it over the line.

There were screams and shouts at the front of the house.

"They're hee-re!" Ma shouted.

"Lovely."

Grandma reached into her basket, grabbed a handful of fabric, and pulled, still jabbering. I wished they taught

Russian at my school. It would have been more useful than poetry.

The blender revved up in the kitchen, and Aunt Joan sang the chorus from "Margaritaville". Ma and the others cackled.

Grandma shoved her fabric at me.

"Let me finish the baby stuff first," I said, pointing to my basket. "Then I'll take care of yours. And I'll turn the sprinkler back on. Maybe I'll join you. Maybe I'll drown myself in your baby pool."

She frowned, grabbed my arm, and forced my hand into her basket.

"Geez, pushy, aren't you? Okay, okay, I'll hang up your undies, keep your hair on."

I pulled out a mountain of fabric, all kinds of chiffon, silk, satin, cotton, and gauze in every shade of pink. I shook it out.

It was a dress, a ball gown with a plunging neckline, an even deeper scooped back, a small waist, and layers of skirts that flowed to the ground.

"What the hell—?"

Grandma grabbed my shoulder. For a withered elf in a bathing cap, she had World Wrestling Federation moves. Before I realized what she was doing, she had thrown the dress over my head, prodded my boobs into place, spun me around, and zipped me up.

I twirled as quickly as my sore toe would let me. It was the weirdest freaking dress ever. Hands down. The skirts swushed and swirled around like I was in a dream or a shampoo commercial. It fit perfectly and was as soft against my skin as my favourite sweatpants.

"What did you do?" I asked.

137.

The screen door slammed open.

"Ohmygodohmygod!!!"

My aunts poured out of the house shrieking at full volume, a flock of flying dinosaurs landing in a circle around me.

"Will ya look at that!"

"A beauty, she's a freakin' beauty."

"Mary Alice, come look at your beautiful daughter!"

Ma came down the steps slowly, one hand on her belly, eyes wide. She screamed, "Oh, my baby! My baby Ashley is growing up! Ow!"

She sat down on the steps. Her real baby had given her a good, hard kick from the inside to shut her up.

"Stop screaming, Mary Alice," Aunt Sharon said. "You always make such a scene."

Aunt Linny walked around me, her mouth hanging open, tears in her eyes. Aunt Joan felt the fabric.

"Where did you get it?" she asked me.

"I guess Grandma Shulmensky made it. I mean, I think she did."

"I'll be damned," Ma said. "Twirl, Ash."

I twirled again, slowly. The skirts caught a little breeze and fluttered.

"Jesus, Mary, and Joseph," Ma said. "That's a prom dress. A little weird, maybe—"

"Not weird, original," said Aunt Sharon.

"Original like Ashley," added Aunt Joan.

Aunt Linny looked confused. "But Mary Alice said you couldn't go to the prom. That's why I made fudge and brought the tequila."

"I still say you should sue," said Aunt Joan.

"We were gonna make margaritas," Aunt Linny continued.

"To help drown our sorrows," said Aunt Sharon.

Ma stood up, waddled over to me, and smoothed down my skirts. "No margaritas for anybody. My baby is going to the prom. I mean, look at this dress, for crying out loud. It was meant to be. I'll talk to the principal, get an exemption. Something. Anything."

I turned my back to her. "Unzip me."

While Ma fumbled with the zipper, her mouth shifted into high gear. "Linny, she needs a better bra for this. Joanie, could your friend Pely come over? What time is it, almost six? Forget Pely, we'll do her hair ourselves. A loose bun, maybe. And we'll curl the tendrils, what do you think? God, this zipper is stuck something awful."

"Tug harder," I said. "I am not going to the prom and

I am not spending the rest of my life in this dress."

"Shut up, Ashley Marie, you are absolutely going to that prom. This dress is a sign from God."

Ma and her sisters paused to cross themselves.

Great. Now the prom was a sacrament as well as a pain in my butt.

They all started talking a million miles an hour about shoes and a purse and hairpins and curling irons and if it was possible to find a date who happened to own a tux in the next fifteen minutes.

I got so distracted by all the hands futzing with my dress and my hair that I didn't even notice Aunt Joan reach down the front of my dress. She grabbed my tube top and yanked it over my head. The dress stayed where it should, thank God.

"Voilà. She don't even need a bra!" Aunt Sharon cackled.

"She don't need a date either," added Aunt Linny. She pinched my cheek. "She's perfect the way she is."

"Speak of the devil and he appears," said Aunt Joan.

138.

TJ rolled into the backyard wearing a slightly too big black suit, a black shirt, a red necktie, and red high tops. My aunts whistled. Ma's eyebrow arched up.

"Hey," he said.

"Why are you dressed like that?" I asked.

"Your dad made me," he said. "I already returned the damn tux, so he said I had better find a suit."

"Why? We're not going to the prom."

"No, but we're going out. You look hot, babe, way hot. Fine." He reached out to touch me.

I stepped back. "We're going out?"

"To a restaurant."

"Another big night at Burger King?"

Grandma Shulmensky spit on the ground, muttered something, and went into her house.

"No, honey," my mother butted in. "You're going on a nice date. Our treat. Your dad got you a car, too."

"Surprise!" shrieked Aunt Linny. She pulled a camera out of her pocket and snapped a picture. The flash blinded me.

"What's going on?" I asked.

TJ blinked, too. "Did he say what kind of car it was?"

Ma checked Aunt Sharon's watch. "He should be out front by now. Go take a look."

A white Cadillac was purring at the kerb in front of the house. Dad opened the driver's door, cut the engine, and got out.

"Wow." He looked me up and down, and up and down again. "Wow."

"Go ahead," Ma said. "Spin."

I spun, sort of. The dress flowed over the grass like the wind. Aunt Linny snapped away with her camera.

"Wow, princess," Dad repeated. "Wow."

"You already said that," I pointed out.

TJ circled the car, looked in the windows, and whistled. My aunts jiggled up and down, squealing.

I turned back to Ma. "This is real? You did all this for me?"

She shrugged and folded her hands over her belly. "Maybe."

TJ coughed. "Maybe? They said if I didn't take you out to a nice place tonight, I'd never get to see you again."

Aunt Linny gave Ma a hug. "Ain't she great?"

"What about this car?" I asked. "We can't afford this."

"I had a friend who owed me a favour," Dad said. "Let's leave it at that." He tossed the keys to TJ. "Any scratches or dings and your legs will get broke, so take it easy."

"No pressure," TJ muttered.

Dad slipped his hand around Ma's back. They looked so cute for a second I wished they were the couple going off in the white Caddy.

"Hold on," I said. "Did you get Grandma Shulmensky to sew my dress, too?"

Ma shook her head. "Nope. That one has me stumped. Maybe she's a mind reader or something."

"You were supposed to wear one of the dresses we got for you," Aunt Linny said. "They're still in my car. Imagine our shock when we got here and you were dressed up and ready to go."

"She's not quite ready," said Aunt Joan. "Go put your face on, kid."

It took me four minutes to pin up my hair in a sexy bun and put on foundation, blush, eyeliner, mascara, and Eternal Passion lip gloss. There was no point in trying on any shoes. I wasn't going to the ball, and besides, my toe hurt too much. I put on my slippers, checked my teeth for lipstick, and hiked up my boobs.

I gave myself the once-over in the mirror.

Not bad. Not too shabby for a normal kid.

Maybe Nat was right. I did deserve a night out.

Let the fairy tale begin.

I began my float down the stairs like a video diva, or a princess – no, a queen. Ashley Hannigan, Queen of the Not-Prom.

That's when my mother screamed loud enough to break windows in a three-block radius.

I picked up my skirts and hobbled down the stairs as fast as I could. Ma was so pale her freckles looked green.

"She's gone!" She held up an empty can of ravioli. "Grandma escaped!"

Ma took charge of the phone to alert the neighbours. I sent the aunts to check out the surrounding streets. Dad's job was to watch Ma and make sure she didn't do anything stupid like go into labour.

"What if she was hit by a car?" I asked TJ. "What if she got kidnapped, or she fell and she can't get up?"

"Calm down," TJ said. "She's a hundred years old. How far could she go?"

"She's a little weird. She could be in Delaware by now."

"She probably went home to take a nap," he said.

"That's right!" I grabbed his hand and kissed his cheek. "You're right! She went home!"

"Your mother already checked," Dad said.

"We'll look again," I said. "Grandma can be sneaky."

We checked all the closets, the attic, and behind every box in the basement. Nat's bedroom still smelled like nail polish. Grandma's room smelled like soap and cinnamon. I froze there for a second in the doorway. Her sewing machine was on a folding table in the corner of her room, with fabric scraps from my dress and old-fashioned heavy scissors.

TJ came up the steps munching on a pastry he took from the kitchen.

"What?" he said. "I can eat and look at the same time, can't I?"

Ma was hanging up the phone when we walked back in.

"Anything?" she asked.

"Nothing," I said. "You?"

"No one's seen her. Your aunts are still looking. I'm gonna call the cops."

"She's been missing for fifteen minutes. Cops won't get involved until she's gone for twenty-four hours," Dad said.

"That's for normal people," I said. "They'll search right away if it's a crazy old lady."

"Especially if you tell them she can bake," TJ said, licking the sugar off his fingers.

"I think we should tell Yevgeny and Natalia," Ma said.

"You're overreacting, Mary Alice," Dad said. "This ain't good for you. Just relax, okay? She'll be back before you know it."

"What is wrong with you?" Ma yelled. "That poor woman is out there alone and lonely—"

"Hold it!" I stepped in between them. "I know where she is. Grab the condoms and get in the car."

"The old lady needs condoms?" Dad asked.

Two minutes later, we were headed for my school in the white Caddy. Ma rode shotgun. I was stuffed in back like a forgotten piece of pink Kleenex.

"This is a real hot date," TJ muttered.

"Don't be an ass," I said.

"What is it with you?" he asked. "First you love me, then you hate me, get a tux, take the tux back. Now we're tracking down the old kook..."

I flicked the back of his head with my fingers. "Shut up and drive."

"Hey," he yelled. "I'm just saying."

"Don't yell at my kid." Ma slapped him upside the head. "And step on it."

142

As we pulled into the school driveway, TJ had to slow the Caddy to a crawl.

"Damn," he said.

"Yeah," I said.

Stick enough limos in a parking lot, and even Carceras can look classy. Crowds of parents and friends lined the sidewalk that led up to the front door. The dressed-up, glammed-out prom couples strolled down the sidewalk, smiling for the cameras and waving to their fans. It was our very own red carpet show.

"Are you sure she's here?" TJ asked.

"Pull over." I grabbed the cardboard box. "We'll get out. You park and meet us at the door."

I got out first and helped Ma. That baby of hers was getting bigger by the minute. We caught some confused looks as she took my arm and we got in the line of couples waiting to get in. Not many girls take their pregnant mothers to the prom, I guess. Not many show up in their slippers, either.

As we got closer to the door, a few kids recognized me.

"Ashley!"

"Shake it, *mami*!"

"Whoa, girl!"

"Looking good, Hannigan."

Ma pulled my arm closer. "Let's cut to the front of the line."

"We can't. It's too crowded. And don't you dare pull the 'baby's coming' routine again. Nobody will care, trust me. They're here for fun."

The line inched forward. Ma and I scanned the crowd, but there was no sign of Grandma. I knew she was here, knew it in my bones. All of this was coming together in a weird way, like when it was done, it was going to make sense, but we weren't quite there yet.

A minute later, TJ joined us. "Yo, Ash. We got a problem."

"We got a lot of them."

"I heard that Gilroy is checking tickets at the door. With school security and a cop." He held me back. "We can't let him see me."

"What are you talking about? You dropped out last year. He can't do anything to you now."

TJ ran his hands through his hair, keeping his eyes on the door. "Gilroy said he'd press charges if I ever showed my face again."

Ma was pretending not to listen, but she was catching every word.

"Wait a minute," I said. "We were going to come here, before I got busted. To the prom. How were you gonna get past Gilroy then?"

TJ wiped the hair gel that stuck to his hands on his pants. "I was going to pay a buddy to open a bathroom window so I could sneak in."

"Very sophisticated," Ma muttered.

TJ stepped closer and whispered in my ear. "Come on, babe. Your mother can talk to Gilroy, explain about old Grandma. We'll wait back here, hang by the wall, check everybody out."

The line ahead of us moved and the line behind us pushed. I took a few steps forward with Ma. TJ came, too, his eyes on the door.

"I need to go inside," I said. "I'm sure she's there. She's batty about this whole prom thing, just like Nat. Look at the dress she made, for crying out loud."

"Just explain who you're looking for to the security guards," TJ said. His voice was tight.

I held the box up. "I want to sneak these in, too. The security guards won't like that."

TJ wrapped his arms around me and blew gently in my ear. "Let 'em get their own damn protection. You and me have better plans for that box. Come on, babe."

"Let go of me," I said.

TJ squeezed tighter. "You don't want to be a part of this shit." He nibbled my neck and whispered. "I want to get you out of that dress."

I peeled his arms off me and stepped away.

"Hello? Are you crazy? I do too want to be a part of this 'shit'. And I'm keeping the dress on, thank you very much."

He rolled his eyes.

"You don't like it, you can leave," I said.

"Maybe I will."

"Maybe you should."

"Maybe I'll find somebody else to take home."

"Knock yourself out, asshole." I grabbed Ma's arm. "Emergency!" I shouted. "We got an emergency here!"

Ma and me butted and barged our way to the front of the line. TJ fell back into the shadows.

"About time you told him where to get off," Ma said.

The security guards stood in our way.

"We're looking for an old lady," I said. "I know she's here."

"We don't got old ladies here," the first guard said, eyeing my mother. "This is the prom."

"Watch it, buster," Ma said.

"What's in the box?" the second guard asked.

"Her medication," I said.

"Right. That's a good one. Go home now."

"No, listen—"

Mr Gilroy stepped in between the two guards, a sick ferret smile on his face.

Damn.

"Miss Hannigan. I was afraid of something like this. You are determined to force a confrontation, aren't you?"

The kids behind us pushed a little, complaining about the delay.

"Mr Gilroy, it's not what you think. Let me explain."

"Miss Hannigan, you have three seconds to get off school property or I will direct this officer to escort you. We will then press charges."

"That's it!" Ma shoved me to the side. "All right, you weasel. I've had a hard day. Shut your yap and listen."

The crowd behind us went silent. Kids at Carceras can smell a good fight for miles.

"Madam, can I help you?"

Ma bellied up to Gilroy, got right in his face and let it fly. All those years of watching Court TV were not a waste. She told him we were to look for a frail, dying Alzheimer's patient, that the police were on the way, and he was standing in the way of us saving her life.

The crowd started whispering.

Then she told him that he had been a creep when he was her social studies teacher back in 1988 and he was still a creep today, only now he was pathetic and twisted, too.

The crowd giggled.

Ma said that our lawyer was filing a lawsuit against Gilroy, Banks, the superintendent, and the school board for singling me out for cruel and unusual punishment. That she was going to see him fired and yank his pension. If she had her way, he'd be pumping gas by Christmas.

The crowd broke into applause. I almost did, too, but she shot me a warning look.

"Now." She whipped out her extra-long Ma finger and shook it in his face. "You are getting the hell out of our way, and we are going inside."

Gilroy stepped to the side.

A car screeched to the kerb, the driver leaning on the horn. Everybody turned around to look.

"Oh, crap," Ma said.

It was Dad's taxicab. He leaned out the window and waved at us. "We found her!!"

Grandma Shulmensky leaned over, waved a can of ravioli, and blew kisses with her free hand.

"A touching family reunion," Gilroy said. "Anything else you'd like to say, Mrs Hannigan?"

144.

That's when we should have left. Grandma was safe. We'd explain everything to Nat and her dad. If we were lucky, we'd figure out a way not to get sued by Gilroy for public humiliation and slander. I'd kiss and apologize at every red light and do other things with TJ to get him to forgive me. We still had the Caddy and I still looked fine. We could drive east to Atlantic City and sit on the beach until the sun came up, me still wearing my beautiful, strange gown.

Conversation started up again and the music in the gym got loud enough for us to hear at the door. The show was over; folks wanted in. The crowd behind us pushed forward, and the security guard started checking their tickets and letting them step around us and pass through the metal detectors.

The old Ashley, the normal me, would have walked away. Well, limped away, listening to Ma complain, helping her into the car, putting up with TJ sticking his tongue down my throat while my parents argued, and keeping Grandma out of trouble.

"Are you okay?" Ma asked. "You look kinda funny. Your stomach acting up? I'll make you toast when we get home.'"

145.

Once upon a time there was a girl who decided to make it happen.

146.

"I'm going in," I said.

"What?" Ma squinted and leaned forward. "What did you say?"

"I'm going in. I want to dance with my friends."

"What about TJ?"

"TJ who?"

She stared for second. The crowd pushed forward again and blocked Gilroy's view of us.

"You can't go in there," Ma hissed. "Gilroy wants to arrest you. Me, too, probably."

"Seriously, Ma, I'm going in."

She pried my right eyelid all the way open and stared at my eyeball. "Are you high? Dammit, Ashley, if you got high with TJ, so help me God—"

I stroked her cheek once and put my finger on her lips.

"Straight as an arrow, Ma, listen. You always wanted to see me at the prom, right?"

"Been dreaming about it since you were born."

"Here's your chance. Plus, you get to use your acting skills in front of a huge audience. I need a distraction. You know..." I waved at her belly.

She put her hands on her back and stretched a little. "You really want me to do this? You won't be embarrassed?"

"I didn't say that. Just make a distraction."

She sighed. "Lord knows I'm good at that. All right. Work your way over there to the left and hide the box of you-know-whats. The things we do for our children, I swear..."

I kissed her forehead. "Thanks, Ma. You're the best."

She let out a groan. Then a louder groan. She clutched the guy in a hipster tux next to her. He backed off like she had smallpox, but Big Mike Whelan (looking very sharp in a bow tie) stepped forward and caught Ma as she fell towards him. Ma turned the groan up to a wail.

"The baby's coming!"

I let the security guards and Gilroy rush by me, then slipped behind a group of girls wearing saris. I turned around just before I snuck in the door. Ma had Gilroy in a hammerlock and was shrieking in his ear.

"The head! Mother Mary, have mercy! I can feel the head!"

She winked at me and I took off.

Hollywood lost a great one when my ma decided to drive a bus.

No way. That is not the gym. Not our gym.

It was a miracle; Nat's crazy pink notebook come to life. The bleachers, the basketball nets, the BEHAVIOUR AND CONSEQUENCES poster – they had disappeared in the dark. The sky was filled with twinkling white stars, the walls covered with waves of purple and silver. There were rows of round tables (with white tablecloths!) and chairs to my right and to my left. The refreshment tables were along the back wall, with the English teachers, stars in their eyes, standing behind it. And in the spotlight at the centre of the gym was the dance floor, with speakers at the corners and the DJ cuing up music at the back.

I looked behind me. No guards. No Gilroy.

I picked up my skirts and mingled with the crowd.

Nat must have rented a couple hundred out-of-work celebrities, because none of the people sitting, walking, leaning over to fix a corsage, flirting, smiling, sipping orange soda out of a plastic cup – none of those people looked like they went to school with me. They were dreams in suits and tuxedos, visions in silk and chiffon and lace. Skin glowed in the light from the candles and the stars, teeth sparkled, rhinestones turned into diamonds, and everybody was in love.

Monica was the first person to see me.

"You're here!" she screamed. "You're here! I got down to one thirty-nine and my dress fits! I'm so happy. Isn't this awesome?"

"Look at you," I said. Monica, who normally wore her shorts too short, shirts too tight, and earrings ghetto-big was gorgeous in a peach-coloured gown that clung to her best assets – boobs and waist – and skimmed over the rest like it didn't matter. Her hair was long and curly. I had never seen it out of a ponytail before.

"You like it?" she asked.

"You're rocking the whole house in that thing," I said.

She grinned and nodded. "Yeah, I know." She touched her pearl earrings. "These were my mom's."

I swallowed hard, blinked away my tears and gave her another hug. "Gorgeous."

"Okay, that's enough," she said, fanning her face. "I had to put on fresh mascara two times already. Damn earrings always make me cry. Come on!"

She grabbed my hand and dragged me through the crowd to a table in the back corner. The entire prom comm was there looking like beautiful flowers, the kind you see in expensive vases in hotel lobbies. When they saw me, there was screaming, hugging, jumping up and down, and a final round of screaming. I looked around, worried that

Gilroy and his goons were going to notice the commotion and drag me away, but groups of girls were doing the exact same thing all over the gym while their dates stood back and watched.

"Look at that dress!" Lauren said.

"Where did you get it?" Junie asked.

Aisha tilted her head like she was doing mental math. "Where did you get the money for it?"

I explained that a neighbour sewed it for me. My cheeks hurt from grinning so much.

When they got done staring at me, they took turns showing off. I barely recognized any of them.

Lauren's dress looked like a layer of gold skin poured over her. Aisha had on a short grey dress that sparkled in a million directions every time she moved. Junie had on an old-school prom gown: light blue satin, fitted bodice with spaghetti straps and a floor-length skirt plumped up by thick layers of netting. Lauren's hair was pulled back in a sleek bun, Aisha's was braided with thin silver ribbon, and Junie's was crimped and oiled. I checked Junie's left hand but she wasn't sporting a diamond so I didn't say anything about Charles.

The DJ started playing background music, not fast or loud enough to dance to. Around the gym, heads started bobbing, hips swaying back and forth.

"Here comes Nat!" shouted Junie.

Mr Shulmensky rolled Nattie over to us. The whole

screaming, hugging, jumping thing happened again, except that Nat couldn't jump; she could only hop on her butt in her wheelchair. Mr S. joined the English teachers at the cake table. Nattie's eyes looked a little crossed. For sure she took that second pain pill.

We pushed Nat to the closest table and all sat down. I put the cardboard box under my chair. They fired a million questions at me about my dress and my foot (the slippers did stick out a little), and how I got in.

Finally Monica looked around and asked, "Where's TJ?"

I shrugged. "I don't know and I don't care."

Nat pumped her fist in the air. "Yes! She sees the light – woo-hoo!"

The DJ grabbed the mike.

"Are you ready to party?" he shouted.

Everybody rushed the dance floor. Charles, Ramon, and Jamel came to escort their ladies. The first beats out of the speakers were so loud they blew the hair out of my face.

A guy who looked like he could be an underwear model, with toffee-coloured skin and hot fudge eyes, asked me to dance.

"She doesn't dance," Nat shouted. Monica pointed to my slippers. "She hurt her foot."

I stood up, laid my hand on the very solid arm of the mysterious, gorgeous hottie. "Oh, no, I feel great. Let's go."

I danced. I really, really danced.

148

After playing six of my favourite songs in a row, the DJ shifted from dance music to screaming thrash crap. My hottie was snagged by a girl whose dress was cut so low she was showing nipple. I couldn't compete with that, so I limped off for something to drink. I waited in line, checking over my shoulder for Gilroy, got two cups of punch, and hurried back to our table.

Nat and I leaned our heads together and I gave her the whole story about how I wound up with the dress and how I snuck in. She cracked up when I told her that Grandma was the magic seamstress.

"That totally explains why she kept trying to fatten you up," Nat laughed. "She kept saying your butt needed to be bigger and that I needed to make you eat ice cream." She laughed again. "You are the only girl here who needed to gain weight for the prom."

"I wish she would have told me," I said. "I would have eaten more muffins."

The music was slow now and a little sucky, to be honest, but that gave us a chance to sit back and check out the rest of our class.

Most of the girls looked great, but when I looked closely I realized there were some skanks mixed in, dressed like rejects from a Britney Spears video. Everybody had kicked off their high heels. The basketball team was wearing shimmering halter dresses that showed off the muscles in their backs. A couple girls were wearing dresses that looked like they cost a thousand bucks. Others were definitely dressed à la Wal-Mart, but they were smiling just the same and looking every bit as pretty. The goth girls had matching protest flowers, droopy dandelions tucked into black rubber bands around their wrists. Their dresses looked like they were stolen out of a graveyard, but they matched their boots, so it was all good.

The men of Carceras really came through for their dates, got to give them that. Fifty different kinds of tuxedoes, top hats, vests, waistcoats with watch chains, shiny shoes, and sunglasses. Something about a tuxedo, I swear. They all looked respectable, responsible, and hot, with their chins up, their shoulders back, the creases on their pants sharp enough to cut paper. I definitely had to distribute the condoms before midnight.

Nat finished her punch and tapped my shoulder. "Get a load of that one." She pointed to Persia Faulkner, surrounded by her perfect popular posse, as usual. The rest of Carceras looked good. Persia and her girls looked like honest-to-God rap divas. Their dresses fit better, their jewellery blinged brighter, and their asses jiggled tighter.

"They've been drinking Chivas all night," Nat said. "Only the best for the Queen Bitch."

"Come on," I said. "Cut her some slack. She's not as bad as you think."

"You're joking, right?"

"No, I'm serious. She helped make this happen, you know. She's been nice to me all week. Watch."

I got up and worked my way through the crowd to Persia. Nat was right. The whole group reeked of alcohol.

"Hey," I told her. "You look great."

The Persia Posse looked me over top to bottom and laughed at my slippers. Some people are so ignorant.

"I love your dress," I tried.

Persia blinked. "You talkin' to me?"

"I just wanted to see how the ride turned out for you guys and to say thanks for helping. You know, the tickets and everything..."

"Who *are* you?" asked one of the Persia wannabes. The rest of them snickered like little dogs.

"I wasn't talking to you," I told her.

Persia leaned forward on her heels. "You're not talking to me neither. Get out my face."

The little dogs in their rhinestone chokers and press-on nails howled.

I limped back to the table.

"What'd she say?" Nat asked.

"She loves my dress," I said. "More punch?"

The next two hours flew by. In between dancing with my girls, my guy friends, my friends who were guys, and a couple potential dates I gave my number to, I helped Nat deal with the behind-the-scenes crap.

Everybody who had a problem came to us. Some needed "official" action. Nat called security about the fight in the courtyard and the rumors of scumbags from a rival high school trying to plant smoke bombs in the boys' room. The little problems were easier: too much orange soda, not enough diet, a cake that wound up on the floor, complaints about the music, girls whose boobs kept popping out of their strapless dresses. We dealt with it all: a few phone calls and five cases of soda were delivered, the custodians cleaned up the cake in a flash, and the girls with the wandering boobs were told to keep their damn arms down – duh. Oh, and I personally yelled at the clueless ho going down on her date behind the bleachers. I mean *puh-leeze, have some dignity.*

The biggest problem was avoiding Gilroy. The girls let everybody know that he was trying to bust me and ruin my night. It wasn't that I was popular or anything, but everybody hated Gilroy so much they wanted to piss him off. So I had a couple hundred spies watching my back. I got used to having my arm pulled to drag me out of sight, or a big guy stepping in front of me, or a total stranger throwing her arms around me to hide me from the vice principal of pain and torment.

The English teachers were way more awesome than I thought they'd be. First, they looked fine, for old people who don't earn much money. They cleaned up real good. Second, they were cool about not interfering with most of what happened on the dance floor and in the dark corners of the room. They let us act like normal teenagers, but didn't let anybody put on a porn show, know what I mean? In fact, it was that really hot teacher who told me about the ho blowing her boyfriend's mind under the bleachers. He thought it would be better if I broke it up than if he did – not so embarrassing for the girl. I didn't think anything could embarrass her, but it was sweet of him to think that.

The third cool English teacher thing was, they didn't narc on me to Gilroy. They didn't like him any better than we did.

One unplanned teacher showed up; our weird old math sub. I ran into him when I was taking delivery of the diet soda at the loading dock.

"What are you doing here?" I asked.

"Trying to sneak in," he said. "I'm not sure how much longer I'll have a job around here. Gilroy's a real jerk."

"Tell me about it."

"Here, let me give you a hand." He loaded the soda cases onto the cart for me. "I promised some of your classmates I'd give them my business card. They're potential clients."

We pushed the cart towards the gym. "So you're here to get people thinking about insurance, is that it?"

"Exactly right, Miss Hannigan. You can never be too careful."

I thought about the cardboard box of you-know-whats hiding under the table. "I have something you could hand out with your card. Trust me, people will remember you. They'll thank you, too. My generation believes in insurance."

150.

After I turned over the condoms to the math sub, I saw Gilroy headed my way. I hurried over to the photography corner to hide. The photographer had set up with his digital camera and big lights, taking pictures of couples for a little cash. I stood behind the background curtain until I got the signal that Gilroy was gone.

The music stopped. "Okay, okay, okay," the DJ said. "I need everybody to clear the dance floor please, except for, ah," he checked a piece of paper in front of him, "Charles Fournier and Junie Yoo."

"Here." The photographer passed out disposable cameras to me and the other kids standing near him. "I heard this was going to happen. Use these for candid shots. Give them back to me at the end of the night."

Yeah, Charles did it. In front of everybody, girls

236

squealing, guys rolling their eyes, Junie shaking like the first leaf that falls in October, Charles suddenly looking ten years old, he got down on one knee in the middle of the dance floor, and pulled out a ring with an itty-bitty diamond chip in it.

"Will you marry me?" he asked, his voice cracking.

I think Junie said "Yes." It was hard to tell because she was crying so hard. Camera flashes exploded all over the gym, and a wave of girls with stupid ideas about rings with itty-bitty diamonds in them crashed onto the dance floor. I wanted to raise my hand and say "Excuse me, don't you think you're a little young, you still watch Cartoon Network," but then Gilroy popped up again, so I ducked out into the back hall.

151.

"There you are, missy." It wasn't Gilroy, thank God. It was the head custodian. "You got a problem."

"I took care of the soda that we ordered," I said. "And I locked up the loading gate like you said."

"I thought we had a deal," he growled.

"We did," I said. "We do. Are you talking about the money? Nat will pay you at the end of the night."

"You break the deal and we walk off the job. We walk off the job and old Gilroy will shut down this dance."

"It's not a dance, it's a prom. What are you talking about?"

I couldn't believe it. There I was, having the best night of my life, and a guy with a push broom was shaking me down.

In the twinkling lights he looked like a tired, disappointed owl. "Follow me."

We walked out the back door of the gym towards the locker room hall. I kept close to him with my head down. The custodian went into the girls' locker room with me right behind. He took me past the lockers, past the coaches' office, to the bathroom door.

He opened it.

The smell hit me like a slap in the face.

Oh, no. Not tonight. Not in this beautiful dress, please God, I'm begging.

The custodian leaned towards me, his eyes bigger than ever. "Our deal was no vomit clean-up. A deal's a deal."

He turned and walked out, sweeping as he went. I took a deep breath and stepped inside.

The smell and the sound were unmistakable.

Persia Faulkner was on her knees worshipping the porcelain god. In the stalls on either side of her were two of her wannabe friends. All three of them were puking their guts and their Chivas Regal out.

And I had a camera in my hand.

How could I resist?

I shot the entire roll of film, group shots and close-ups. Then I had my own deal for Persia and her girls.

"Clean up this mess and I'll give these pictures and negatives to you on Monday. Screw up and I share them with the whole school."

I was good.

152.

I went straight to the dance floor and joined in. We were all shaking it, spinning, sexing, slinking, shouting out, raising the roof and bringing down the house. There was love on the dance floor: Monica and Mark; Leeann and Big Mike; Quong and Danny; Dalinda and Ian; Junie and Charles; and Lauren, Aisha, Nat, and me.

The whole committee danced around Nat's wheelchair, and then the songs came faster and faster, and the heat turned up, and we were moving, moving to a beat never heard before in the halls of Carceras High School, arms waving, hips popping, hearts locked into the same rhythm, the same beat, until we danced so hard I thought for sure we were going to float all the way to heaven.

153.

Everything was perfect right up to the minute the cops arrested me.

154.

By the time I stood in front of the night court judge, it was almost morning.

The officers had been real nice to me, because I wasn't drunk or high or a bitch. The tall one who found me a jacket when I got cold said he felt bad about the whole thing, but somebody from the school had pressured the chief of police so they didn't have a choice. He told me he had been named the king of his prom, out in Denver, but that his date left with his best friend, so the night had been a bummer. He hoped I had a better time.

I said I did.

Natalia's dad called around, and I wound up being defended by another Russian. We have a lot of them where we live.

Ma showed up, too. She waved at the judge when he walked in. Turns out they went to high school together, and the judge's sister had been on the softball team with Ma and Aunt Linny. The judge couldn't stand Gilroy's social studies class, either.

He dismissed the charges and told me my dress was very pretty.

Mr Shulmensky drove us home just as the sun came up over New Jersey. We got to the top of a hill and had to stop at a Wawa so Ma could use the bathroom. No way was she gonna make it home, she said. Mr Shulmensky said no problem, he wanted to get a newspaper and a cup of coffee anyway.

I got out and leaned against the car. There were a few clouds in the sky. Maybe they had been partying all night, too. Out in the west, towards Pittsburgh, the moon was setting, pulling a couple stars down with it. I liked how it was all happening at once, the moon and stars pinking up in the sunrise, the whole world spinning around like it was supposed to.

156.

Once upon a time there was a girl who got a life.

157.

Me.

How It All Turned Out

Getting back to regular school after the prom was what you call extremely, horribly, ass-kicking hard, but I did it. Everybody did. We showed up to our classes, all us normal kids who for a couple hours had been masters of our universe. We woke up when the alarm rang, put on clean clothes and brushed our teeth, and walked through the Carceras metal detectors for all those last days in May and June. We studied for finals, most of us, and dragged our butts to class and took the tests. We passed.

I passed.

Nat got an awesome financial aid package from Temple, and a bunch of scholarships. She only has to take out a little loan, so when she gets her college degree, she won't be killed with payments for forty years. She decided to stay home and take the city bus down Broad Street to Temple. That's one of the coolest things about living so close to Philly. The bus will take you anywhere.

As we got ready for graduation, the flowers in Nat's grandmother's garden bloomed like nobody's business. That old lady definitely had weird juju stuff in her fingers, crazy Russian magic or something. The roses were as red as fresh blood and as fat as a fist. I didn't know the names of the other flowers, but Ma did. She'd sit in a lawn chair next to the fence with her feet propped up on a tricycle or laundry basket and watch those flowers grow, fifty shades of pink and yellow and purple. Her belly kept growing, too. We had a pool going on the size of the baby. If I won, Ma was going to be in the Guinness record book, for sure.

The weekend that Nat and Mr S. moved Grandma into the nursing home, Ma cut all the flowers. I helped her arrange them in vases and plastic buckets, then we drove to the nursing home and filled Grandma's room with colour. Then I drove Ma to the hospital at twice the legal speed limit.

My little sister, Adrian, was born in the entrance to the emergency room.

159.

It was Adrian who helped me figure everything out.

Ma was on the stretcher talking about birth control to the banged-up thugs who had just watched her give birth. The doctor checked out Adrian, wrapped her up, and handed her to me. I only had her for a second; you know how hospital people are. But it was the longest second of my life. Hers, too, I'm sure.

She looked like a prize fighter; kind of bloody, a bit

confused, eyes swollen and blinking. I cleaned off her face with a corner of the blanket. She reminded me of me: a little on the scrawny side, red hair, pale skin, and blue eyes.

Those eyes opened wider. She looked right at me.

Wow.

I decided to move out of my parents' house.

Talk about a sucker punch. It hit me like a left hook out of nowhere that moving down to the basement would totally suck, and moving into a rat hole with someone like TJ would suck even more, and I had to find another way out of there, but I didn't want to go too far, because this little girl needed me to show her the ropes and all.

When they took Adrian out of my arms, she cried.

That was cool.

160.

So we got through all the hospital stuff, and Ma and Ade came home. We had a combo graduation and new baby party and saved a ton of money on food and drinks. Ade was a hit at the party. She peed up a storm and wailed loud enough to be heard over the music, which was good.

I sprung my big idea on Nat and her dad the first time I took Adrian to visit Grandma Shulmensky. They were cool with it. So was my dad. Ma took a little extra convincing, but Aunt Linny pointed out that I'd be close, and Aunt Sharon said it meant I could babysit for Adrian when Barry Manilow came to town, and Aunt Joan told Ma to shut up and let me have a life.

TJ, well he tried. He sent me cards, he sent me beer. He came around to my graduation party with roses, but it was over, dead and gone. Don't know why I stayed with him so long. What a waste. I heard that he moved some chick from Cherry Hill into the slimeball apartment, and I'm just counting the days before she turns up pregnant or he gets his first felony conviction or both. I never did find out the name of his sister's baby.

It's a little weird now, paying rent to Mr Shulmensky and living down the hall from Nattie, who always leaves a mess in the bathroom. I don't care if that cast is still on her leg, how hard is it to hang up your towel? And to be honest, I'm nervous about this whole community college thing, though Nat keeps telling me it'll be way better than high school, 'cause I'm in charge of me, and if I don't like it, I can always quit, which no way I'm gonna do, because I'm paying for all of it, and you'd better believe I'm gonna get my money's worth.

I'm taking Liberal Arts classes for now. It doesn't mean, like, drawing or painting kind of art, or being a liberal like in politics, which is what I thought the first time I heard it. It means I want to learn a few things before I decide what I want to be. It's too bad they don't give degrees in prom management. Accounting sounds kind of interesting, because at least when numbers don't add up right, you can figure out where you went wrong. I even thought about maybe becoming a teacher's aide, or even a teacher some day. I know a few things about normal kids.

Hell, I could write a book about them.

Acknowledgements

Many, many, many thanks to the members of my personal Prom Court who stood behind the creation of this book—

Prom Queens

Stephanie and Meredith Anderson, for letting me take over the couch and for keeping me supplied with popcorn.

Jessica Larrabee, for being so patient with me.

Sharyn November and Regina Hayes, for constant cheerleading and support.

The women of the Bucks County Children's Writers Group, for riding the roller coaster with me.

Amy Berkower and the staff at Writers House, for taking care of business.

Sarah Henry, for saving my sanity.

Prom Kings

Christian Larrabee, for letting me write during that awesome blizzard.

Scot Larrabee, my husband, for absolutely everything.

251

Special Mention

A loud, rowdy shout-out to all the "normal" kids who talked to me the last couple of years and told me nobody ever writes about them. Hope you like it.

The Music

This book was written to the tunes of Beethoven, Bruce Springsteen, Coldplay, Eminem, Norah Jones, and Sting. And, of course, the tunes of Y100 in Philadelphia.

WINTERGIRLS

Cassie and Lia did everything together, including staying thin. But then Cassie died. Now the voice in Lia's head tells her to stay strong. Lose more. Weigh less. Thin. Thinner. Thinnest.

"Brilliant, intoxicating, full of drama, love and, like the best books of this kind, hope"
Melvin Burgess, *OBSERVER*

NEW YORK
TIMES
BESTSELLER

I
WASN'T
SICK,
I WAS
STRONG

WINTERGIRLS

LAURIE HALSE ANDERSON

CATALYST

Kate's life is sorted. Until it all goes wrong. Kate splits up with her boyfriend and gets rejected from the only college she applied to. Her life is spiralling out of control – and Kate's about to find out how exciting that can be.

From the
BESTSELLING
AUTHOR of
WINTERGIRLS
THIS
WAS
NEVER
THE
PLAN
CATALYST
LAURIE HALSE ANDERSON

TWISTED

Tyler has gone from geek to popular boy overnight. Then he's accused of a terrible crime. He didn't do it – but will anyone believe him?

From the
BESTSELLING
AUTHOR of
WINTERGIRLS

IF
THEY
SAY IT,
IT'S
TRUE

TWISTED

LAURIE HALSE ANDERSON

LOOKING FOR JJ

Three children walked away from the
edge of town one day – but only two of
them came back...
Alice Tully is trying to put her past
behind her and move on. But the past
has a way of coming back – and it could
rip her new life apart. A beautiful 10th
anniversary edition of an award-
winning novel.

Winner of the Booktrust Teenage
Prize 2004.

"Compassionate, unsensational and unflinching" *The Guardian*

ANNE CASSIDY

LOOKING FOR JJ

"DARK, CHILLING AND CLEVER" *CELIA REES*

LITTLE GIRL MISSING

10TH ANNIVERSARY EDITION

CLOSE YOUR PRETTY EYES

Olivia is going into her sixteenth care home. It's her last chance for a family. But then she discovers the house is haunted. The danger is real – but how much of it is coming from within? A stunning psychological thriller from an award-winning author.

"A sensitive and powerful novel"
Daily Telegraph

"A complex book that emphasises the power of love"
Literary Review

Sally Nicholls

CLOSE YOUR PRETTY EYES

"A writer of enormous power and strength"
Literary Review